Open to Love

A Novella By
Lyndell Williams

After Hours Publications

Lyndell Williams

Open to Love by Lyndell Williams
©Published by
After Hours Publications
www.afterhourspublications.com
All Rights Reserved

Opent to Love is a work of fiction. Names, characters, places, and incidents either are the product of the author's imagination or are used fictitiously. Any resemblance to actual persons, living or dead, events, or locales is entirely coincidental.

Any unauthorized reprint of use of this material is prohibited. No part of this book may be reproduced or transmitted in any form or by any means, electronic, or mechanical, including photocopying, recording, or by any information storage without express permission by the publisher.

Warning: This book contains explicit language and adult themes suitable for ages 17+.

Edited by Foolproof Editing

ISBN: 9798627740065

www.laylawriteslove.com

Table of Contents

We Need to Talk 5

Eviction 13

Little Boy 21

First Date 27

The Qureshis 35

Ghusl 43

Polygyny Fight 51

Drawer Space 55

Wedding Night 63

New Bed 71

Tell Him 81

Sketchpad 85

New Things 93

Ibrahim Qureshi 101

Bonus Reads 111

   Turning Around 115

   Something Special 123

   My Way to You 151

   Sweet Love – Bitter Fruit 165

We Need to Talk

ALL THINGS CONSIDERED, HAFSAH had the second wife thing down. She tugged open the oven door and bent her head towards the aromatic heat. Juice streamed past the cloves of browned garlic stuffed inside the leg of lamb. She smiled at the hunk of meat. "Alhamdulillah, perfect. He'll love it." She grabbed her phone from the counter and dialed as she sashayed through their pristine apartment smelling of all-purpose cleaner and incense. She stopped in front of the mirror and teased out her black coils. She couldn't suppress the self-satisfied grin smiling back at her. She was, in fact, the bomb.

"Hi, you've reached Mahmoud Abbas—"

"Damn it, where is he?" she grunted, bumping into the small round table and knocking over a stemmed glass. "He promised." She cleared her throat before the voicemail recording ended. "As-salam alaykum, Moodman. I'm just wondering where you are." She set the glass aright and straightened the silverware on cloth napkins as she spoke. "You should've been home an hour ago. It's been a long week, and you got a hot meal and wife steaming over here." She sucked her teeth and shook her head as she hung up. It was corny, but

Mahmoud liked mess like that, so she learned how to leave sexy messages and texts while they were apart.

She massaged the space between her eyes, flopping on the sofa dominating the great room. The silk of her African print caftan cascaded over her. She had ignored all the horror stories sisters in the community incessantly droned into her ears. Unlike many of them, she didn't consider polygyny a big deal. It was halal, and Mahmoud made it clear that he had enough money for another wife. She spied the name *Tarika* on her phone's screen. "I'll call her later." After hitting the red button, she checked the time before laying down and tucking a pillow under her head. It was late. That was the frustrating thing about her marriage and life—everything seemed to happen late—leaving her to do nothing but wait.

Waiting was what she was doing before Mahmoud. As she worked her way through her twenties, she was bombarded by people pestering her with warnings that she was becoming an old maid. At first, she paid them no mind, but then thirty came and went. Everyone ratcheted up the pressure, and she began to feel the need for companionship. So, when her Arab suitor came calling to woo her with all of his fineness and smoothness, the choice was easy. She shivered and curled against the cool leather while her lids fluttered closed.

* * *

"Hafsah? Habibti?"

Open to Love

Hafsah took a deep breath and moaned. The enticing scent of Mahmoud and his cologne made her tingle from head to toe. She opened her drowsy lids and gazed into her husband's gray eyes. "As-salam alaykum." He smiled and held his bottom lip between his teeth.

Hafsah stretched and smiled. "Wa alaykum salam. What time is it," she asked, running her fingertips up his brown long-stubble beard and through his hair. So handsome. She couldn't stay mad at him.

"A little after midnight." He slipped a strong hand under her gown and up her thigh. "I'm sorry. I got trapped at the office and left late. He hovered his mouth over hers. Her nerves sparked through her body. "Forgive me?"

She pulled his lips to hers. Any semblances of irritation evaporated under his touch. His hand roamed to her bottom and squeezed. She turned her head. "Okay," she gasped. Mahmoud lifted her and sat on the sofa, setting her on his lap. "Moodman." She held onto his broad shoulders. Warm nips to her neck made breathing even harder. He always knew exactly where to touch to send her reeling. "Don't you want to eat?"

He met her gaze. "Yes." He leaned her backward.

Her stomach growled. She giggled and straightened. "I meant food." She shot off of him and strode into the kitchen. She pulled the cold hunk of lamb meat from the oven and dropped it onto the kitchen island. She sighed. "So much for the romantic dinner, I planned."

Mahmoud shrugged out of his leather jacket and dropped it on a kitchen stool as he sat. "It's fine, Habibti." He plucked up a chunk of meat and chomped off a little. He held the rest in front of his lips. "Delicious, just like you. I can't wait to eat both." He winked and shot from his seat. "I'm going to change. I'll be right back."

She watched his round bottom as he strutted into the bedroom. Coming or going, Mahmoud Abbas was fine. While cutting the lamb, a phone rang. She jumped and looked down. Her heart kicked up a notch at the name on the screen of Mahmoud's cell. It was her. She rolled her eyes and stabbed harder at the meat. "Here we go." Whenever Moodman is here, she has to keep callin'." She turned and took a plate from a cabinet. Her phone was next. Her lungs constricted as she read the words *Our Little Blessing* on the screen. The plate shattered on the floor. She heaved as she read.

Afaf: *As-salam alaykum. I was too excited to wait. Did Mahmoud tell you about our little blessing?! Alhamdulillah, our family is growing.*

A blurry black and white image popped on the screen. Hafsah's heart pounded in her chest, threatening to fall to pieces next to the dish at her feet. Mahmoud was having a baby with his first wife?

"Okay," Mahmoud clapped his hands as he strode out of the bedroom wearing a tank and pajamas. "Let's eat, then we can get onto dessert." He sat back at the counter.

Hafsah took in as much air as she could. Glaring at her husband, she slid the phone across the counter. "Is there something you want to tell me, Moodman?"

Mahmoud rubbed his forehead and said something in Arabic. "She shouldn't have done this." He rounded the counter. "I'll talk to her."

Hafsah backed away from his open arms. His first wife pulled a bitch move to stick it to her, and it was working. "You're having a baby with Afaf? What happened to not wanting to have children? You told me you weren't ready."

He stepped closer. "That's not entirely true. I—" Mahmoud yelped and hopped on one foot across the room. "What is this?" He sat on the arm of a side chair and picked at the bottom of his foot.

She stepped over the mess. "You'll live." She stood over him, poking his shoulder. "Answer me. I went on the pill because you said you didn't want children. Now Afaf is pregnant?"

"I said that I didn't feel like *we* should have kids." He plucked a tiny shard from his foot and stood. "I still don't." He cupped her face. "I want you to myself."

She slapped his hand away. "So, it's not that you don't want to have kids. You just don't want to have them with *me*. You sneaky son of a—"

"Enough. I'll not have you using such language. I was going to tell you about Afaf, but I just wanted to enjoy time with my wife." He brushed past her.

"But I guess that isn't happening. Why are you even upset? It's not actually any of your business."

Hafsah froze where she stood, staring at Mahmoud as he reached for the pan and started eating lamb like he hadn't just dropped a massive bomb on her. Was he right? Did she really not have any business knowing what happened with his other family? After all, it really didn't affect her life.

"By the way," he said between bites, "I'm going to need you to prepare to move to the city. Afaf will need me around more, and I can't keep taking the trip all the way out here." He bent his head back and dropped a hunk of meat into his mouth.

"Excuse me? I'm not moving to the city. I gave up nights so I can stay near my parents. She gets to be with you all week. Isn't that enough?" She wanted to cram the next slice of lamb down his throat herself. Things were going great. Now he was changing everything—Afaf's pregnancy, moving? It was all too much.

"Not anymore." He motioned her to him with a finger. "Don't worry. I found you a nice little apartment in Soho."

She crossed her arms. "No."

Mahmoud bolted and grabbed her chin. His eyes flamed with rage. "You're my wife. If you expect me to be a good husband, you have to learn when to just listen." He slammed them shut and inhaled. He smiled and rubbed her arms. "Come on, Habibti, don't be difficult. He drew her closer and nuzzled her neck.

Open to Love

She wanted to melt into his arms. To forget everything but the two of them. He drew her closer and moaned. Her body exploded in a rush of burning desire. She truly loved and wanted him, but at what cost? She held in her gut and pushed him away. "I said no." She braced herself on the counter. "I'm not sitting in an apartment in the city all alone. It's not like I'll ever get to go around your parents and relatives. They haven't asked me to one gathering in the entire year we've been married."

He came behind her. "It's because you live so far away. There's another reason why you should move."

"Oh, please. Your parents have a house in the Hamptons. So, they can drive there but can't seem to accept any of my invitations? No, and we both know why. I'm not your wife in their eyes. Isn't that why you're perfectly fine with having kids with Afaf but not me? I'm just a temporary thrill, not a real wife, right?"

She searched his face, praying for him to tell her that she was wrong. He averted his gaze but not quickly enough. She saw it clearly. He agreed with her. She was such a fool to fall for his routine. She was nothing more than a plaything.

"I—of course not. I just think we should wait for a while." The slight tremble in his voice gave away the fact that he was lying through his teeth.

"How long is a while?"

"I don't know."

"You don't know? Get out," she rasped through the lump of pain stuck in her throat. "I'm not moving to the city to be the halal side piece you get to screw, then go uptown to your real family."

"That's not true. You're important to me."

"Good," she wiped her palm across her wet cheeks, "then we'll stick to what we've been doing, and you'll make it work."

He sighed and dipped his head. "I can't do that." He held her hands. "You have to move to the city. If not. This isn't going to work."

She closed her eyes and pressed her forehead to his. She had already made so many concessions to make him happy. How much more was she supposed to give up? The tight-knit African American community she grew up in meant everything to her. Her friends and family were not going to be sacrificed. "Then it won't work out."

Mahmoud jerked his head up and stared at her. The shocked expression on his face screwed into anger. His cold glare sent a chill down her spine. "Fine," he spat out, pushing her away. He jerked his jacket off the stool before grabbing his phone and keys.

He slammed the door shut, and Hafsah's heart finally joined the plate on the floor—just as shattered and broken.

Eviction

HAFSAH FLOPPED ON THE BED AND held the phone to her ear. Electric anger surged through her nerves with each ring. She stared into the open closet across from her. Mahmoud's side was bare. He tried his best to cajole her into bed the night they fought about her moving to the city. When she made it clear that she was having none of it—and he was having none of her—he packed his belongings and slammed the door behind him. Not that there was much for him to take. Just some casual clothes, a toiletry bag, and hair trimmer. "Come on, pick up, you lying son of a bitch." The tight muscles at the base of her neck burned harder at the sound of a female answering. Just great.

"*Can't you leave my husband alone?*" Afaf's soft shrill grated into her ear. "*He doesn't want' you.*"

She closed her eyes and took a deep breath. Putting up with Afaf's hateful words, all the years of her marriage was bad enough. Hearing them during her divorce waiting period was just too much. A verbal catfight with her soon-to-be-ex-co-wife would only waste time. There were bigger things at stake. "As-salam alaykum, Afaf. I need to speak to Mahmoud."

Lyndell Williams

"Didn't you hear me, whore? He's through with you." Afaf sputtered Arabic into the phone.

Hafsah pressed her lips. The words she was able to understand were not something a good Muslim woman should say. The witch was coming close to being cursed out. "Listen, Afaf—" The line went dead. "Nice—" she took the phone from her ear and looked at the screen"—petty bitch." She hovered a thumb over the call icon. If only she could finally be done with Mahmoud. She looked at the words FINAL NOTICE in red letters on the paper in her hand. No such luck. She pressed the button. More Arabic vulgarities flowed into her ear. "I know he's there." She scrunched the paper in her hand. "Tell him if he won't talk to me, then I'll have to contact my father." A lawyer was what she needed. She should have never trusted him. Mahmoud's base voice joined Afaf's. They began shouting at each other. Hafsah smirked. Guess her refusal to melt into the abyss of co-wives lost put a kink in their lives.

"Hafsah," Mahmoud seethed. *"What do you want?"*

"I got a notice that the rent still isn't paid."

"And it won't be. You're one of those strong Black Muslim women. Take care of it yourself."

She shot off the bed and began pacing. "You can't do that. It's your obligation to pay the rent until the iddah is over. You have to pay for last two months and next month."

"Well, I won't, not for there. I have a beautiful apartment for you here in the city. It's bigger and

Open to Love

closer to my work. Move, and you won't have to worry about anything."

"Why would I move to the city now? You're divorcing me."

"*I don't have to.*" Her heart quickened at the softness that had seeped into his tone as Afaf's yelling faded and disappeared after a soft click. "*We could stay married. I don't want this divorce, and neither do you. All our problems can be solved if you just pack your things and come to me. I miss you so much, Habibti.*"

"You're unbelievable."

"*Why? Because I don't want to lose my wife? I miss you so much, having you in my arms.*"

She took a deep breath, fighting back the butterflies his sultry voice blew into a tizzy in her gut. "You're the one who pronounced talaq." Her voice trembled with her insides. He was so sexy. She closed her eyes, visualizing his handsome face as he spoke.

He chuckled. "*Nothing is set in stone. I'll call the imam and tell him we're reconciling. It can be good for us here. You'll be close to my work, so I can see you more often. You can make new friends. I bought you that nice new car. Use it to drive back and forth to visit your parents.*"

She opened her eyes and walked to the window. She pulled back the striped drape and allowed the rays of sunlight filtering through to warm her and steel her resistance. He could be so manipulative, tapping into her emotions to get her to do anything he wanted, but not this time. She clenched a fist.

"No. I've given into you more than enough already. I'm tired of catering to your ego and every need. If you want me, you'll get in your car and come here. I'm not moving."

"*Then you're not getting your rent paid. You may choose where to live, but I decide how I spend my money.*" There was another soft click, this time shutting *her* out.

"Asshole!" Her screech at the ceiling bounced off the walls of the bedroom. Her cheeks began to itch from the tears streaming down them. The sound of the teapot whistling wafted through the door. She took a deep breath and walked to the stove and poured a cup before smoothing the notice next to her tablet shining on the counter. She balanced on a stool, cradling the cup between her fingers. It was given to them as a wedding gift, one of the few proofs that she was married. The warm sensation running through her fingers but not the chill from the reality that she built a life with a man who considered her no more than some fun and sexual kicks while he was away from his real family. She sniffed back a few more tears and took a sip.

Her mother's face lit up on the phone screen. She groaned and cleared her throat. "As-salam alaykum, Ma."

"*Wa alaykum salam. I'm checking to see how you are. You haven't called for a couple of weeks. Your father is ready to come over there.*"

She slumped her shoulders and sighed. "I'm sorry. I'm fine."

Open to Love

"*Are you sure? I know the divorce is hitting you hard. Are you eating?*"

"Yes."

"*Sleeping?*"

"Come on, Ma. I'm all right." She let out a nervous chuckle, rubbing her forehead. Hiding anything from Ma was almost impossible, but letting her know about the rent would lead to a demand that she moves back home. That wasn't happening. Ma and Dad were great, but the independence was too sweet. She had to keep it and spent the next half hour dispelling any concerns that she wasn't fine before her phone beeped. "Someone is on my other line, Ma. I gotta go."

"*Okay, As-salam alaykum.*"

She returned her mother's salams before clicking to the other line. "As-salam alaykum, Tarika."

"*Wa alaykum salam. How did things go with Mahmoud?*"

She massaged a temple. "Subhanallah, not well at all. He refuses to pay any bills unless I move to the city."

"*What? For real? He put you in iddah but somehow wants to stay married?*"

"He expects me to give up and go running to him and do as I'm told."

"*You're not, though, right? I know how in love you are with him, but he only thinks about himself.*"

"Don't worry. I love myself more. I was ready to be a second wife, but I won't live my life trailing behind someone who only sees me as a piece of ass."

Tarika chuckled. "*Girl, you're a mess. I know you do. Allah blessed you with too much to waste your time chasing after some man. Your iddah is almost over anyway. You'll just have to start paying bills earlier.*"

She took another sip of tea and looked around the large room. "Yeah." Independence wasn't cheap. "I guess I will."

"*You can handle it. So, what's next?*"

"Job hunting. I was so dumb to quit my last one to play Susy Homemaker."

"*Quitting wasn't a mistake. You always said you wanted to be a stay-at-home wife and mother. Mahmoud was the mistake. Besides, you have your dowry to keep you afloat.*"

"I do." She slid her fingers on the tablet's surface. Her bank balance shone on the screen. Not an exorbitant amount but enough to survive until she found a gig. "Alhamdulillah, I wasn't so taken in by Mahmoud's games that I didn't demand an acceptable dowry like so many other sisters." Sure, she had been a fool, but at least she wasn't a broke one.

"*See, silver lining.*"

"More like brass, but I'll survive. Let me go and find a job. As-salam alaykum."

"*Wa alaykum salaam.*"

"Bismillah." She clicked back to the employment website and restarted the search she was doing before she had to call Mahmoud about shirking his responsibilities. Hopefully, finding a job was going to be easier.

After reading through a ton of descriptions, she arched her back and moaned. "Come on. There must be something." She poured another cup of tea and scrolled some more. Maybe there wasn't.

Little Boy

HAFSAH'S ARMS ACHED as she struggled to organize the massive sheets of paper at her desk. Her new job at the firm was a Godsend. Mahmoud made sure their divorce was a nasty one. He had refused to pay rent or any bills during the iddah, forcing her to drain her dowry while searching for a job. By the time the three-month waiting period was over, she had barely a penny to her name.

She swallowed back the painful memories and continued to move the papers. Once she had her workload in a manageable state, she flopped in her office chair. "It's gonna be a long day." Her phone lit up. She squinted, clenching her teeth as she read.

Mahmoud: *As salama alaykum. We need to talk.*

"Unbelievable." She started tapping the screen.

Hafsah: *New phone. Who's this?*

Mahmoud: *You know who it is.*

Hafsah: *Does your wife know you're texting strange women?*

Mahmoud: *Come on, Habibti.*

She fiddled her fingers, thinking of a nasty of enough response. Her best friend's face appeared on the screen. She smiled. "As-salam alaykum, Tarika."

"*Wa alaykum salam. What's up?*"

"Well, Mahmoud has been texting me."

Tarika gasped. "*For real? He has his nerve after the way he treated you. Does he think you forgot all the games he played just because you didn't want to deal with his foolishness?*"

"I know, right? We agreed that I would stay on the island and he would commute from the city. Then after knocking up his first wife, he decided that he couldn't make the trips to see me. I'm not even trying to give him the time of day."

"*Good. He was lucky you accepted being a second wife anyway. Besides, there are plenty of brothers in the community asking about you.*"

"I'm not giving them the time of day either. They just think I'll be co-wife again. That's not happening."

"*So, you're not interested in anyone at all?*"

She scoffed, "No one at all."

"As-salam alaykum, Hafsah." She jumped and looked up. Faheem Qureshi smiled down at her. Despite her attempt to not let them, the twinkle in his brown upturned eyes made her insides melt. "I had lunch out today." He held up a black plastic bag. "I remembered that you liked this place when we worked on the Dawson project, so I got you something."

"Oh. Jazakallah. You didn't have to do that."

"*Who's that?*" Tarika asked.

He looked down toward the floor with a sheepish smile. She opened the bag and let out a small squeak. "Oh, I love steamed dumplings." The schoolgirl demeanor was shameful but couldn't be helped.

"*Whoo izz that?*" Tarika asked again with an increasingly agitated tone.

"Enjoy." He swaggered away. She bit her lip and enjoyed the show, glad that the opening of her cubicle faced his office.

"*Hafsah.*" Tarika's voice blasted through the phone.

She ran a finger between her *hijab* and chin. "That was Faheem, one of the architects. He brought me lunch."

"*Oh, really? That was nice of him. He must be pretty fine the way he had you sounding all flirty.*"

"He's alright, and I didn't sound flirty. I told you, I'm not looking for a husband."

"*Mmm-hmm. So, what's his background?*"

"He's Desi. His father's parents are from New Delhi, and his mother is from Uttar Pradesh. He was born and raised here though."

"*You found out all that about him, but you're not interested?*"

"He told me while we were working one day. It's not a big deal."

"*Girl, you're lying to yourself. I know you better than that.*"

"Okay, I'll admit that he's fine and nice, but he looks so young." She spied him, reaching for his door while reading a book. "I can practically smell the breast milk from here."

Tarika's laugh drifted through the phone. "*You're insane. As-salam alaykum.*"

***

The rest of the workday went, as usual, save the awkward glances they shared that made her mind whirl. *He was only trying to be nice. He gets lunch for other people. Could he be interested in me? Do I want him to be?* Her desk phone rang. She tucked it under her ear and continued to roll the large sheet in front of her. "This is Hafsah Brooks."

"*As-salam alaykum, Hafsah.*" Heat rushed up her neck at the sound of Faheem's voice. "*I'm interested in getting to know you better outside of work.*"

She crushed the sheet against her chest and stared at the wall-sized window to his office. "Oh?"

"*I would like to have your wali's number.*"

"Wow. You expect a lot for some dumplings."

His low chuckle made her tingle where she shouldn't. "*No, I've wanted to ask you for a while. I've heard a lot of good things about you.*"

"You've been investigating me?" She tried to feign shock but couldn't get rid of the damn girlish twitter in her voice.

"*A little.*"

She lifted a corner of her mouth. "Then, you know how old I am?"

"*I do. You're thirty-five.*"

"And how old are you?"

He cleared his throat. "*Not thirty-five.*"

"Younger?"

"*Yes.*"

Open to Love

"Okay, tell me your age, and I'll consider giving you my father's number." She held her breath, hoping he was at least the legal drinking age.

"*I'm twenty-six, but—*"

She dropped the phone on the receiver. Grabbing her handbag from the drawer, she walked past the cleaners vacuuming and emptying out dustpans. The little boy had his nerve. It was time to head home.

"Hafsah," He called from behind. She picked up her pace towards the lobby. "Please, just hear me out." He walked ahead and turned in front of her.

She gazed up. His boyish grin was gone, eyes gleaming with determination. "You're too young for me, Faheem."

"I don't think so."

"We're at different places in our lives."

He sighed, running his fingers through his long curls. "I'm already a junior architect and working to make partner." He pulled out his phone. "Look, here's my house. I'm renovating it, so it doesn't look like a palace—not yet."

She took the phone and swiped through the pictures. "It's beautiful."

"I may be young, but I'm established. Now, I want to find someone to share everything I've built. I thought it might be you."

She braced herself and stared back at him. Why did he have to be such a snack? "Alright, my father's number is," she blurted out the numbers as she rounded him and dashed out of the door.

"That's not fair."

She hopped into her car and pulled out of the parking lot, rubbing at the pit of guilt in her gut as she merged into traffic. Maybe she should've given him a chance. *Oh, well, it's too late now. He'll probably give up.* She reached for the radio when her father's ringtone chimed through the speakers. She tapped the green phone icon. "As-salam alaykum, Dad."

"*Wa alaykum salaam.*" Her father's deep voice filled the car. "*How are you?*"

"Alhamdulillah."

"*Good. Listen, I just got a call from a young man named Faheem. He says you know him from work.*"

"Yeah." She felt a rash of goose pimples burst on her arms. "I know him."

"Well, he just ran down all of his qualities to me, and I have to say, I'm impressed. He appears to have his head on his shoulders. He wants to place intentions on you. What do you think?"

Unbelievable. He had remembered the numbers. Perhaps he wasn't such a little boy after all. She had underestimated his determination to get closer to her. It was time to let him. "I'd like that." She turned the handle. Headlights beamed into the darkness. Things were getting brighter.

First Date

"I'M SO PATHETIC." hafsah crossed her legs at the ankles and shook her foot while checking the time on her phone. It was way too early. She had spent the few weeknights since they got engaged, putting together the perfect outfit, so she was fully dressed and fidgeting by the time her father arrived to chaperone them on their first date in respectable Muslim fashion.

As strange as it was to get ready to meet another man in the home, she started with Mahmood, her nerves tingled all day. The hours passed so slowly. "Look at me," she raised her hands and flopped them on the sofa, "I'm sitting here all thirsty." She passed a thumb over her freshly manicured fingertips before spreading her palms over her crisp new full-length skirt. Everything had to be new—clothes, shoes, even underwear—nothing once worn during her previous marriage. Change was happening.

Her father laughed and reached for his steaming cup of tea on the coffee table. "Not at all. It's usual to be excited about your intended." He put the cup to his lips and tilted his head back.

"I don't know," She rose over her father and held out her hand. "This isn't my first time doing this. Why am I so nervous?" She took his empty teacup and walked to the kitchen.

"Thank you. It's your first time with Faheem." He combed his fingers through his graying beard as he leaned back in the side chair. She watched him close his eyes and rub his close-shaven head with a serene face. "Inshallah, you two will be fine."

She raised her brows. "That's a change in attitude," she said while filling her father's cup, "you weren't nearly so sure about Mahmoud."

"Mahmoud was a different story. Everyone I spoke to about Faheem said he was a good guy—well mannered, into the Deen—and he seems sincere about his feelings for you."

A loud engine rumbled through the window. She turned and leaned over the sink. "Is that him?" She strode to the door and opened it. Her heart thumped a little faster at the sight of Faheem climbing out of a humongous black pick-up with giant tires. The white long-sleeve top he wore hugged his muscles in all of the right places. She shifted her gaze to the walkway.

"As-salam alaykum," he sung, holding up a huge bouquet.

"Wa alaykum salam." She tucked them into the crux of her arm and ran a finger across the burst of yellow. "These are so beautiful. How did you know I liked sunflowers?"

"You're welcome," her father said before laughing and hugging Faheem. "As-salam alaykum, Faheem. It's good to finally meet you face-to-face."

Open to Love

"Wa alaykum salam, Brother Amin." Faheem patted her father's back with his palm. "I agree."

Amin lay his arm across her shoulder. She gazed up at him, searching for his response to meeting another suitor. Ignoring her father's ability to read people in the past was a mistake not to be repeated. The serenity remained on his smiling face as he chatted. This was something new too. He had been much more guarded with Mahmoud.

Her father dropped his arm. She rounded her suitor and looked at the monstrous truck oozing testosterone. "Wow," she sighed and passed a hand along the warm black hood before looking in the open bed. Two-by-fours laid across the back, peaking under a tarp-covered with building materials. "I never pictured you in something like this."

"Well—" Faheem approached "—I take my car to work during the week and drive this on the weekends. I hope you don't mind." He smiled.

She giggled. "Not at all." How was he able to throw her so far off her guard? The bitter divorce hardened her to the game most brothers ran. She was not usually in the mood to be wooed, but Faheem Qureshi was different.

"Nice toolbox," her father exclaimed on the other side of the truck, tapping the shiny metal box straddling the bed.

"Alhamdulillah, thanks." His broad chest expanded even further as he leaned on the box. "This helped me pay for school. Now, I use it to renovate my house."

Her father's grin widened. "You worked your way through college?"

"Yes, sir, in construction under my uncle. He is a master carpenter. I work my way through everything." His tone brought every nerve to attention. He always cut a smart and confident figure, but this new level of smoothness was completely disarming. She met his gaze in hopes of showing him he wasn't all that. Things only got more hopeless. Staring into his sparkling eyes, the staunch Muslimah inside of her swooned. He dangled keys in front of her. "Would you like me to jump in the back so you can drive?"

She swallowed and bit her bottom lip, wanting more than anything to press them against his full, luscious ones. "Yup." She grabbed the keys. Tossing the flowers in the back, she hopped in the driver's seat.

Her father sat in the passenger's seat. "Impressive rack." He stroked the metal gun rack hanging from the roof. He beamed at Faheem as if he was already his son-in-law. A lot of help he was going to be on taking a hard line with her intended. "You hunt?"

"Not lately," said Faheem climbing onto the seat behind her. "I don't have the time with working on the house. I do try to get to the range a couple of times a month."

"You're an enthusiast?"

"Yes, and an NRA member. Muslims need to be able to protect themselves."

Open to Love

"Mashallah, agreed. Plenty of people ready to point their guns at us. You should come by my house and check out my collection, inshallah."

Turning the ignition, she rolled her eyes and let out a sigh. "Subhanallah, don't start, Dad," she scoffed, fastening her seat belt.

She looked in the rearview mirror at Faheem's knitted eyebrows. "You're anti-gun, Hafsah?"

"No. I'm anti-bore Hafsah to death talking about firearms."

Her father let out a guffaw. "Don't worry, Faheem. My baby girl can lock and load with the best of them. She has excellent aim."

Faheem reached between the front seats and leaned on the console, tilting his head toward her. "Indeed, she does. Do you need help?"

He winked at her, all cocky. He would have to pay for that. She slowly blinked and put the truck in gear. "No, I got this." Pounding her foot on the gas, she made it jerk backward. He muttered in a foreign language and chuckled. "Seat belt, brother." She stopped the truck.

Their lips came dangerously close to touching. He straightened and cleared his throat. Mr. Smooth was obviously feeling the intense energy surging between them too. "Yes, ma'am." He grabbed the front seat, leaning forward until his head was close to hers. "Let me put the address in the GPS. Then all of us can talk." His breath brushed her cheek. Her nipples hardened under her hijab. A throbbing sprang between her legs. Alhamdulillah for chaperones.

"Yes," her father injected in a serious tone, "let's talk." Faheem sat back and fastened his seatbelt. He handled her dad's grilling during the car ride with the same finesse she'd seen him use at work. He was straightforward and asked questions of his own. By the time they arrived at the restaurant, the two men were talking like old homies.

Once inside, they followed the greeter through rows of diners eating and chatting at their tables. Faheem held out a chair for her. Her father turned to the waitress. "Excuse me, I'll need my own table next to this one." Her heart kicked up a notch. He'd never given Mahmoud this amount of liberty. Dad was clearly team, Faheem.

Sitting at an adjacent table, her father pulled out his phone and began tapping the screen. She squeezed her knees and met his gaze. As much as she'd wanted to be alone with him, the limited seclusion had her head pounding. He was so close. "I guess it's my turn to ask questions." She scratched the back of her head through her hijab.

He flashed a gorgeous smile. "What do you wanna know?" Her list of questions and requirements cascaded from the back of her mind and into a glob of letters lumped in her throat.

"Umm—" As easy-going as Faheem seemed, he was still a man—a Muslim one—and previous "sit-downs" with potential spouses taught her that they did not like the women they courted to have a lot of expectations or ask too much. Things might turn ugly. She hadn't pressed Mahmoud, which led to her disastrous first marriage. Could avoiding the same mistake mess things up with him?

"How about," He lifted the menu in front of him, "we order first? I'm in no rush." He cocked a brow and glanced at her. "Although, I may have to take my car in for new brakes—the way you were ridin' them."

She gasped and hit his side of the table. "I was not." Their shared laughter dissolved the tension twisting at the base of her neck. Her father had asked almost everything listed anyway. Why not sit back and have some fun? She flipped open her menu.

The Qureshis

"Alhamdulillah, dinner smells great, Mom." Faheem stood behind his mother in front of the stove full of steaming pots and pans. Mom was no joke in the kitchen, and she obviously went all out for their special guest. "Hafsah is gonna love it." He reached over her shoulder and plucked up hot salmon croquette.

Dara elbowed his side. "You quit it, Faheem. Leave something for your intended."

Laughing, he pecked her cheek and strode into the hall, stopping in front of the mirror. He combed his fingers through his hair and smoothed his eyebrows before passing a hand down his burgundy shirt. It was Hafsah's favorite color, something he learned during one of their many dates.

The first one went off without a hitch. Of course, there was another as well as a string of chaperoned weekend excursions. The roar of his truck into Hafsah's complex became an expected sound. The space in front of her door was honorarily reserved for him by the neighbors, who he charmed once they decided to stay at Hafsah's townhouse while he finished the house. Staying in the home she shared with another man wasn't ideal, but hunkering down with either of their parents was out of the question.

His father jogged down the stairs. "Don't worry son," he said while passing him and heading into the kitchen, "you look like a Magazine cover. She won't be able to resist." Faheem watched him strut up to his mother, looking up at her before kissing her round, brown cheek. "You've done it again, Dara." He rubbed her bottom.

"Alhamdulillah. Thanks, Rami." She put a spoon to his lips. Her lips soon followed.

Faheem looked up at the ceiling and scoffed. What a floor show. "You two, don't start. Hafsah will be here soon. She doesn't need to see my parent's pawing each other."

"You zip it, Son." Rami passed a hand over Dara's hair. "This is my house and my wife. I'm enjoying both."

"Exactly," she chimed and put another spoon of food to his lips. Faheem shook his head. It was useless. They were always this way. There was a knock at the door. "I got it." His stomach bubbled as he padded through the house in his bare feet. His heart flipped at the sight of Hafsah's smile. "As-salam alaykum." He stood to one side. "You look great."

"Wa alaykum salam, thank you." The evening breeze following her inside made the skirt sway at her ankles. She kicked off her shoes next to his. "I'm sorry I'm late. GPS was not kind to me."

His mother's laughter filtered into the room. "It never is." Dara glided down the hall and gave Hafsah salaams before hooking an arm around hers. "I'm so glad to finally meet you. Your name is all I've heard for weeks."

Rami followed. "Don't embarrass the boy, Dara. As-salam alaykum, Hafsah. I'm Faheem's father. Let's all go sit." He held up his hand towards the living room.

"So, Hafsah, Faheem told us you were married before?" asked Dara, settling into the crook of Rami's arm as they sat on the mocha grey overstuffed sectional. Faheem sighed and sat as close to Hafsah as he dared on the attached chaise. His mother didn't pull any punches. She had some unanswered questions. Dara Qureshi did not like having unanswered questions.

The smile faded from Hafsah's face. "Yes, for a couple of years." She tucked at the hijab fabric under her chin. "It didn't work out. We wanted different things."

Dara knitted her eyebrows. Faheem bit his bottom lip and looked between them. Hafsah was the best woman he had ever met. If his mother had any reservations, it would hinder their plans. Her divorce didn't bother him, so it shouldn't be an issue for anyone else. Dara pressed her lips together. "I see. We've taught Faheem to be open and honest. I hope you don't mind if I am?"

"No." Hafsah slid her hands up and down her skirt. He inched closer, resisting the urge to throw his arms around her.

"Rami and I find your age difference and previous marriage, let's say, disturbing. Faheem is young, and this would be his first committed relationship."

Hafsah folded her hands on her lap and straightened. "I understand."

"Hafsah and I already talked about her previous marriage, Mom." He puffed up his tight chest. "I'm not bothered by it."

Mom perched on the edge of the sofa, squinting at him. "That may be, but divorces can be very painful." She looked at Hafsah. "Was yours?"

"Yes—" Hafsah dipped her head "—it was. I've been seeing a counselor and focusing on healing. I wasn't looking to get married again, but Faheem can be very convincing." She lifted her head and smiled at him. The pressure in his chest relaxed. She had this. "I thought it might be too soon, and I did worry about our age difference, but I'm confident we can have a good marriage, inshallah."

Mom's stare didn't falter. "Faheem persuaded you? So, you know the things he wants?

"Yes, and they are the same things I want. To share our lives and build a strong Muslim family, inshallah. He's determined—"

"Stubborn." Mom pat Hafsah's hand and chuckled, turning her head to Dad, who smiled and nodded. "No need to mince words. We know our son."

Hafsah started laughing and reached for Mom's hand. "Subhanallah. He can be but not always." She beamed back at him. "He listens to my side most of the time, except when it comes to sushi."

Faheem lifted his chin. "It's bait. I'm not eating bait." The women burst into a fit of giggles.

Mom volleyed more questions, all of which Hafsah answered with confidence and grace, not a surprise. Eventually, she rose and offered Hafsah a hand. "This one can be a handful, just like his father. If he gives you any trouble, let me know." She put an arm around Hafsah. "Let's eat." The women walked out of the room.

Faheem caught his father's gaze. Rami smiled as they rose from the sofa. "Looks like your mom is taken with her. I like her too."

Dara guided Hafsah to a seat right next to hers. "Sit here, Hafsah," she said, pulling out the chair. She tapped his shoulder. "Come and help me in the kitchen."

"Okay, Mom." He followed her.

She turned and kissed his cheek before lifting a sheet of aluminum foil from a large platter on the counter. "I like her."

"Alhamdulillah." He wrapped his arms around her round shoulders. "You don't know what that means to me."

She nudged his side. "Stop, Faheem. Help me get this food on the table."

"Yes, Ma'am." He lifted the platter and waltzed into the dining room towards his bride to be.

***

"Alhamdulillah, that was nice." Hafsah stopped in front of her car door. "I love your parents."

Faheem smiled and leaned on the car. "Yeah, they're pretty great. I'm sorry Mom grilled you so hard." He looked down. His fingers disappeared in his soft curls shining in the streetlamp light.

She pulled her keys from her handbag and let out a nervous chuckle. "Don't worry. You gave me fair warning that your mom didn't play games." His mother's third-degree had her stomach in all kinds of knots. Thankfully, Ma had prepped her like she was a witness on a crime show. "Not that I can blame her." She dropped the keys in his open palm and met his gaze, smoothing a hand up, and down the goosebumps she felt spring under her shirt. "Her son is quite a catch. Everybody is already wondering why you want to marry an older, divorced woman."

He frowned and lifted from the car, standing in front of her. "I don't give a damn about people. I'm marrying Hafsah, who has been in my head since I saw her sitting all nervous at her desk on her first day at work. I'm marrying a kind, giving person who makes me feel like I can do anything with a smile." He moved closer, forcing her to back away until her bottom met the car. She gasped as he propped a hand on either side of her. "She's who I want and can't wait to hold—" his lips hovered over hers "—and kiss." The shakiness in his voice barely registered through her lightheadedness. Weeks of restraint cascaded down her tingling body, falling around her feet. "Don't ever doubt what you've come to mean to me."

"I won't," she stammered, tucking her hands behind her to keep from grabbing the back of his neck and planting a kiss on his lips. There needed to be more distance. Like hell, was she moving though. "But, Faheem, I do have a past—"

"To hell with your past. I'm your future. I love you, Hafsah. I know you feel it."

The tremble gone, his words rushed over her mouth with his warm breath, jolting the desire torturing her soul. "I love you too, Faheem." She closed her eyes and lifted her chin. *Please. Kiss me. No, it's wrong. Yes, just do it.* His chest brushed her nipples, making each pebble and burn with a need that set her body ablaze with a flame threatening to incinerate her and the world.

"Subhanallah," He rasped and backed away. Air rushed between them, dousing her aching hunger for his touch. She opened her eyes. He stood across from her, rubbing the back of his neck. "I'm so sorry, Hafsah. I just...sorry."

"It's okay." She passed her fingertips over her sweaty forehead and tucked the damp edges of her hijab, gasping for air as her insides shook in protest.

He cleared his throat. "I better get inside," he said, his voice cracking. She smiled. At least she wasn't the only one flustered. He put the key in the car door lock, his hand shaking. "We're going to have to make sure to have someone around until we get married. It's getting hard for me not to—"

he looked at her "—I want you so bad." He shook his head and opened the door. "Sorry." She tilted her head to look in his eyes, but he averted her gaze, his lips tight. Things went from passionate to grim.

"Yes, Astaghfirulullah." She gasped and clenched her clothes. "You need to control yourself, Brother Qureshi. I guess you have to marry me now."

He threw his head back and laughed. "I guess so." She climbed into the car. He bent in front of the car window; a handsome smile spread across his face. "Call me when you get home."

"All right." It felt good to be able to make the man she loved smile. "Faheem."

"Yeah?"

"You aren't the only one having a tough time." She passed a hand back and forth over the steering wheel. "I want you too." No, the hell she didn't just tell him how thirsty she was. Wow, he really had her sprung. He closed the door. She turned on the engine and headlights, hovering her foot over the gas pedal. Better to peel out before saying anything else stupid.

"Well," he leaned closer, "we better get the marriage contract finished as soon as possible. Make sure to get your part done."

The undertone of command in his tone made her insides quiver. She gazed at him, slowly blinking. "I will."

"As-salam alaykum." He stood and sauntered across the street, his cute butt in his jeans taunting her as he walked up the drive.

Ghusl

"COMING!" HAFSAH BENT HER HEAD AND twisted the towel hanging from it. A constant stream of knocking from the front door echoed through the apartment. She rushed through the living room, stubbing her toe on the coffee table. "Ah, son of a…just hold on!" She flipped the towel back and limped to the door. "Dang, girl—" she jerked it open "—is all the banging necessary? I do have neighbors to consider." She glared at Tarika's frowning face before turning. High-pitched wails drifted in from behind Tarika and filled the room.

"Obviously, it is," huffed Tarika as she strode into the kitchen. Rahmah followed, rocking baby Junaid in her arms. "We've been knocking for five minutes." Tarika jerked the refrigerator open and took out two bottles of water. "We're supposed to be halfway to Sister Jenneh's for your fitting by now. You know she hates it when her clients are late."

"I was in the shower."

"You're just getting out of the shower?" asked Rahmah, sitting on a stool and wiping her forehead.

"Yeah, sorry." Hafsah pulled the robe sash tighter and looked at her toes. The memories of her steamy dream about Faheem floated through her mind. It was all his fault that she woke up late.

Tarika rounded the kitchen peninsula and squinted up at the towel perched on her head. "Why are you washing your hair today? You know how much work it is messing with all of that hair of yours."

She avoided Tarika's gaze. "Umm. I had to make a ghusl."

"A ghusl? Why? You had your period last week." Tarika's eyes widened before she burst out laughing and staggered backward. "Damn, Faheem has you that hot and bothered?"

"Shut up." Hafsah scratched the back of her wet neck and crossed her arms. Tarika was too intuitive for her own good. "Did you guys eat? How about you stuff something in that big mouth of yours?"

Tarika held her side and flopped on the seat next to Rahmah. "Don't get snippy with me just because you are all thirsty for Faheem."

Rahmah slapped Tarika's arm. "Leave her alone. She's in love. Just because you swore off men."

"She's horny. I don't blame her, though. You haven't seen Faheem yet. I went with them on a couple of dates." Tarika jutted her eyebrows. "He is all kinds of fine."

Rahmah chuckled. "So, I've heard."

"He has that brown skin with those sexy eyes." Her full lips spread across her heart-shaped face into a smirk. "*And* he has this one—" she pointed at Hafsah "—paying all kinds of attention."

Hafsah took the towel from her head. "I'm glad you approve, but you know, you should be guarding your gaze, sister." She started teasing wet coils with her fingertips. Tarika was right. It was going to take a minute to get this hair under control.

"Oh, I'm guarding it, but it only takes a glimpse to have someone that fine etched into your memory." Tarika fell against Rahmah in a bout of laughter.

Rahmah got up and bounced Junaid, who still refused to stop fussing. "Come on, Little Man. Calm down."

Hafsah walked up and stroked the baby's back. "He's still sick?"

"Yeah. The doctors aren't sure what's wrong."

She looked at Rahmah. Tiny red veins ran through the whites of her oval eyes. "When was the last time you slept?"

"It's been a while. He doesn't stay down for more than a couple hours." Tears blurred the lines in her eyes and wetted her thick eyelashes. The strains of motherhood hadn't dulled her stunning beauty, but she was clearly drained.

"Baaz isn't helping?"

"He isn't in the country." Tarika drank from the water bottle and rolled her eyes. "He flew off to visit the family in Pakistan, forgetting about the one he has here."

Rahmah sighed. "Don't start, Tarika. He'll be back. We'll be okay until then, inshallah."

Hafsah stroked Rahma's arm. "You don't have to come to the fitting. Why don't you go home and rest?"

"No, please." Rahmah wiped a tear from her round brown cheek. "I've been looking forward to this. I spend all day at home taking care of Junaid. I'm going a little crazy."

"Yeah." Tarika stood and held up her arms. "She's been lashing out at everybody. Come to Aunty."

Junaid threw his body back, hitting Rahmah's chin. She stumbled and braced herself on the sofa. "Subhanallah. Just leave him alone, okay? You know how he gets."

Tarika looked at Hafsah. "See what I mean?" There was a knock at the door. Tarika knitted her brows. "You expecting someone?"

"No." Hafsah looked through the peephole and gasped. Faheem stood, holding a food container and with one hand in the pocket of his jeans. He took it out and knocked again. She jumped back from the door. "It's Faheem. What's he doing here?"

Tarika sniggered. "Maybe he's been having nocturnal emissions too."

"Very funny."

"I'm sorry girl. Is he by himself? Because if he is, I'm going to want to know exactly how hot things got last night."

Hafsah clenched the front of her robe. "Not that bad. We almost kissed." Tarika and Rahmah looked at each other before their dubious glances turned her way. "I said, almost." There was another knock. "He put the brakes on it."

"Mmm, maybe he's ready to hit the gas. I'm going to have to remind our Muslim brother that he needs to show some adab." Tarika put her face to the door. "Oh, don't worry. There is another brother with him." She put a hand on the handle.

Hafsah held up her palm. "Wait. I'm not dressed. She scrambled into the bedroom.

"You're a mess," Tarika called out.

"Just answer the door. I can't wait until you're engaged. I'm going to make you suffer."

"Not likely. I'm not down with any of the slim pickings around here."

Hafsah practically slammed the door and raced to the closet, sliding hangers across the rod. What the hell does somebody wear when they're about to see the man they just had a wet dream about? She pulled out a skirt and blouse. Nice and Muslimy. Most people would consider the previous night tame, but no touching ratcheted up the heat. Good thing Tarika and Rahmah were there because keeping her hands to herself would not be easy. He was so kissable. *Down, girl.*

She tugged on her clothes and wrapped her hijab around her head, pricking her finger a couple of times in the rush to pin it. She gazed in the mirror, not flawless but presentable. She opened the bedroom door and walked out with as much grace as her guilt-laden conscious allowed.

Faheem stood in the middle of the living room. He and the broad-shouldered brother standing next to him dwarfed the space. Junaid lay on Faheem's chest, whimpering into a calm from the soft pats on his back. Faheem's calm. He was exceptionally good at it. An aura of promised domestic bliss glowed around him—husband, father of her children. She saw them in him in a way she had never seen in any man before. Fears that he was a rebound faded. Faheem was what she had been looking for in Mahmoud but never found.

He looked at her and smiled. "As-salam alaykum. You look nice."

She dipped her head and smoothed a hand over her skirt. "Mashallah. Thanks. I see you've met Junaid and Rahmah."

Faheem rubbed the baby's back. "Yes. She was nice enough to let me hold him. This is Aqil." He patted the man on a muscular bicep before resuming to soothe the baby.

Aqil turned his head away from Tarika's direction and smiled. "As-salam alaykum. Faheem has told me a lot of good things about you, sister."

"Alhamdulillah."

"We're heading to the range." Faheem pointed to the counter. "Mom asked me to drive some food from last night over, since you liked it so much."

"Aww. That's nice. Thank her for me."

Open to Love

"Will do. I'm sorry to come by unannounced. I tried calling, but it kept going to voicemail." Faheem sauntered up to her, still confident and obviously unfazed by last night.

"Oh, I think I forgot to plug it in last night." She was too busy dreaming about licking every inch of him.

"That explains it." He frowned. "The top of your hijab is wet."

Tarika and Rahmah giggled behind him. She was really going to have to kill those two.

"Everything all right?" asked Faheem with a puzzled look on his face.

"Fine," chimed Tarika. "We have to get going, Hafsah. I texted Jenneh to tell her we're running late."

"The fitting. Thanks, Tee." She reached for Junaid. "I'll take him."

Faheem lifted the now sleeping baby from his chest. "Here you go." Their hands brushed. His eyes flashed, making her heart soar. He let out a nervous laugh. Maybe he was fazed. "We won't hold you ladies up." He made his way to the door. "Come on, Aqil."

"Huh," asked Aqil, looking in Tarika and Rahmah's direction. He ran his fingers through his silky black hair before rubbing his aquiline nose. "Yeah. Nice meeting all of you. As-salam alaykum." He dashed out of the door the moment Faheem opened it.

"Nice seeing you again, Tarika. A pleasure meeting you and Junaid, Rahmah." He pointed to

49

her. "Plug in your phone, Hafsah. I'll talk to you later, inshallah. As-salam alaykum." He closed the door behind him.

Tarika held a hand against her chest and batted her eyelashes. "Yes, Daddy," she said in a breathless tone. "He sure is comfortable taking charge."

"Yes, he is." Rahmah fanned herself. "I'm sure Hafsah is fine letting him too."

"Both of you shut up." They all laughed.

"Now—" Tarika picked up her purse "—get my nephew in his car seat and let's get out of here or else you won't have anything on you when you get married."

Rahmah reached for Junaid and put him in the seat. "With the way he was looking at Hafsah, I don't think Faheem would mind that at all."

"What did I say about shutting up?" Hafsah got her keys from the hook and touched the wet spot at the top of her head. She needed to marry Faheem ASAP.

Polygyny Fight

"Look, Hafsah," Faheem said, smirking with her father as she sat behind piles of catalogs, "how about I focus on getting our house finished, and you handle this wedding stuff?" He leaned back in the chair at her parent's kitchen table. It became his seat during their weeks of courting.

The first date went off without a hitch. A string of chaperoned weekend excursions followed. The roar of Faheem's truck into her complex became an expected sound. The neighbors, charmed by her new beaux, reserved the space in front of her door for him.

She stopped flipping through pages of stationery samples and caught his gaze. *Our house.* He had been talking about them as a couple and planning for "us" and suggesting things "we" should do for about a week. It was nice. She was getting used to it. He winked. An obvious attempt to get her to let him off the hook. It wasn't going to work. Well, not totally. Though she was able to keep a straight face, other areas responded in kind. "Come on, Faheem. Don't be that guy."

"Sorry, but I am." He pulled out his wallet and slid a gold card from it. "If you want me to build a gazebo or something to get married in, fine, but I draw the line at menus and invitations." He pushed the square piece of plastic across the table. "I trust your judgment."

Her father chortled. "Smart man." He pointed to the card as she picked it up. "I'm sure it has the agreed-upon budget."

"Yes, sir."

"Faheem—"

Her mother tapped her shoulder. "Don't bother, Hafsah." Her mother pulled a stack of catalogs towards her as she sat. "Your father was the same way."

"Do you blame us, Saudah?" Her father waved a hand over the table. "Look at all of this stuff."

There was a knock at the door. "I'll get it." She stood and walked to the front of the house, opening it to Faheem's smiling parents. "As-salam alaykum." Dara walked in and gave her a big hug. Rami followed, carrying a huge cake platter. After a flurry of greetings and hugs, the men headed into the living room while the women sat at the table.

"It's so nice to finally meet you, Dara," her mother said with a bright smile.

"Yes, alhamdulillah," Dara said, leaning forward and grinning in kind. "We just love, Hafsah. I'm so glad these two found each other." It didn't take long for the three of them to start flipping through the catalogs.

Open to Love

Two pots of tea and many slices of cake later, they had every detail for the wedding day mapped out. "See," pronounced her mother as she stacked the catalogs on the kitchen island, "it was much easier without Faheem."

Dara laughed. "She tried to involve *my* son?"

The men walked into the kitchen. "What's so funny?" asked Faheem, sitting across from her.

"You," exclaimed his mother before another burst of laughter filled the room.

Her father chuckled and sat at the head of the table, holding a stack of papers. "All right leave my future son-in-law alone. We need to concentrate on finalizing this contract."

"Agreed." Rami sat next to Faheem. "We added each of your stipulations. All we have to do is review them before going to the imam for you two to sign it."

"Yes." Her father kissed her forehead. "Let's get these two married."

Her father began reading through the stipulations, most of which he went through with no interruptions. The expression on Faheem's face remained jovial as he openly looked in her direction. It changed when her father read her stipulation about polygyny. The sparkle in his eyes disappeared. "May I see that?" He knitted his eyebrows, holding the papers in his hands. "I'm not agreeing to this."

She sat straight. "Why not? I told you I didn't want polygyny."

"Yeah, and I understand, but to write it in the contract? You can't make haram what Allah made halal."

"I'm not doing that. I'm just making it clear, and you know why."

He laid the contract on the table. "I'm not your ex—" he poked at it with one finger "—and I'm not going to sign as long as this is in it."

She bolted out of her seat and leaned over the table, mimicking the way he poked the contract. "Fine. So long as you understand that I'm not signing without it."

He stood and glared at her. It was the first time he did, and it ripped her heart into tatters. "Understood. As-salam alaykum." He turned and stormed out of the kitchen.

She straightened and sniffed at the sound of the front door closing. The concerned expressions on everyone's faces blurred behind tears filling her eyes. "Please, excuse me." She raced past her father and up the stairs, flopping onto the bed in her old room. Her heart ached. Her chest heaved. Faheem finally showed his true colors. He was just like all the other Muslim men who were hell-bent on filling their dance cards with as many women as possible. Wiping her tears, she got up and slammed the door, cutting off the voices drifting into her room from downstairs—and her hopes of marrying him.

Drawer Space

HAFSAH YANKED OPEN THE DRAWER AND filled her arms with the layers of folded hijabs inside. She lifted them out, grunting and turning to drop them on the bed. "I have too many of these." Her collection had become downright ridiculous over the years. She picked up one and draped it over her head, looking in the mirror and either smiling and putting it on the top of the dresser or frowning and dropping it in the box labeled *donations* at her feet. It didn't get nearly as full as needed, and the top of the dresser disappeared underneath colors and patterns.

Her phone buzzed. She glanced down, making her heart leap as she read the name *Faheem* on the screen. Holding a hijab closed under her neck, she slid a finger over the screen.

Faheem: *As-salam alaykum. When are you going to talk to me about this?*

She ripped the fabric from her head and flung it on top of the others before picking up the phone and pecking at the keyboard. *Did you sign the contract?*

Faheem: *No*

Lyndell Williams

Hafsah: *Then, there is nothing to talk about. Salams*

She walked back to the bed and picked up a long, crimson hijab. It matched the red lines in her eyes. She tossed it in the box. Enough of both. Her phone rang. "Oh, come on." She glanced at the screen, the name *Tarika* lit across it. Her heart sank a little as she put it to her ear. "As-salam alaykum."

"*Wa alaykum salam. So, are you still crying over your fight with Faheem?*"

"No."

"*Good. Have you talked to him yet?*"

"No." She put the last hijab from the bed in the box and opened another drawer. When did she buy all of these?

"*Come on, Hafsah. You and I both know it's not over between you two.*"

"Maybe it is. He won't sign the contract if the no polygyny clause is in it, and I'm not removing it. I'm tired of giving into men. I don't want to complicate my life with being a co-wife ever again."

"*Did you tell him that?*"

"I told him I didn't want polygyny."

"*Did you tell him why?*"

She scratched the top of her head. "No."

"*Well, that's not very fair to him. How is he supposed to understand how important that contract clause is if you don't tell him?*"

"Whose side are you on?" She picked up the next pile of hijabs and dumped them in the box.

Open to Love

"*Yours. You can't just toss him to the side without giving him a chance to understand how you feel. Faheem isn't like these other shabby brothers out here playing games.*"

"I've let you two spend too much time together."

Tarika chuckled. "*Hey, you said you wanted me to get to know him. Well, I did, and I can see how much he cares for you.*"

She closed the box and smiled. "He told me he loved me."

"*Any jackass can say that. I'm not talking about words. I've seen you two together. He's going to come to you. When he does, tell him how you feel. If he wants polygyny and you don't, it's better to find out now and not end up married with kids when he decides to pull something on you.*"

"I'll think about it."

"*Good and stop moping. Let's go somewhere. What are you doing?*"

She looked at the empty drawers. "Clearing out some drawers."

Tarika's loud guffaw rang out of the phone. "*Probably for Faheem. Face it. You're sprung.*"

She closed the draws and dug the crimson hijab out of the box. "Maybe, but he still has to pay for being such an arrogant jerk and storming out of the house in front of my parents."

"*Agreed. Make sure he comes begging.*"

She covered and dashed to the kitchen counter for her purse and keys. "Oh, trust me. I will. Meet me at Nazar. As-salam alaykum."

Lyndell Williams

***

Faheem leaned against the window frame of his office and blew out a gust of air. Peeking through the white blinds, his gaze fell on Hafsah perched at her desk. Her brown skin glowed from the cream hijab framing her face. She stopped typing and leaned toward the screen, pursing her full brown lips. His itched to finally touch hers. She was so stunning. The wedding was too far away—if it was going to happen.

His phone buzzed. He sprang up and stared at the screen, sinking back into the chair when he read his father's name. "As-salam alaykum, Dad."

"*Wa alaykum salam. Your mother wanted to make sure that you and Hafsah were coming over for dinner.*"

He rubbed his forehead. "It doesn't look like it."

"*I take it that she hasn't come around?*"

"No, and it's been three days."

"*I still don't understand why you two are fighting about this. You never gave me any indication that you would be interested in more than one wife.*"

"That doesn't mean she can put it in our contract. Does she really expect me to sign it? No other wives or I pay ten-thousand dollars each time?" He strode across the office and resumed staring at his fiancé. "These sisters are always complaining about Muslim men trying to control *them*, but then they pull stunts like this. She won't even talk to me. How is she the angry one?"

Open to Love

His father's chuckle streamed through the phone. "*So, you're messing with your happiness because you're mad that she won't let you keep your options open?*"

"It's the principle, dad."

"*What principle? I've watched you when she's around. Your nose is wide open. She's clearly the woman for you. Tell me, did you ever think that you might want to have more than one family?*"

"No."

"*Because it's not for everyone. Brothers treat polygyny like it's an absolute right and proof of their manhood. Many of them just blind themselves to the heavy responsibilities. Do you know why I never got a second wife?*"

"Ma would cut your balls off."

His father laughed. "*True, but that's not why. I decided to spend my life trying to make the woman I love happy and building a solid marriage and family. In return, I get to share my life with a wonderful person. Look, Son, relationships are an investment. That stipulation is a way for Hafsah to feel secure that she can invest in yours. Stop thinking about it as her trying to control you. She's a good woman. Don't lose her over this. Let me know about dinner. As-salam alaykum.*"

"Wa alaykum salam." His father was right. He was never happier than when he was around her. He dialed again.

"This is Hafsah Brooks"

"Hafsah, it turns out I do need something."

She straightened her back and peered across the pool of cubbies, mustering an impassive expression while her legs shook under the desk. "Okay, what?"

Faheem's office door opened. He leaned against the doorjamb and stuck a hand in his pants pocket. "To stop fighting. Please, I'm going crazy knowing I've upset you."

She bit her lips to steel her insides, which his sheepish smile was turning into a pile of goo. "We're not fighting. You shut me down. Is that the way you want to handle our problems?"

"No. You deserve better, and I'm going to work to make sure you get it. If you'll let me."

She lost her battle to stay mad and smiled. His strong arms looked so tempting. She just wanted to melt into and let them soothe her the way his warm eyes did. "Do you want to know why I put no-polygyny in the contract?"

He walked back into his office and closed the door. "Your previous marriage?"

"It was awful. I couldn't go anywhere without someone looking at me funny, including his family. They treated me like I was a ho' for being his second wife. I was able to ignore most of it, but then he changed the rules on me, and when I refused to play things his way, he punished me for it. I ended up with nothing but a broken heart. I don't want to ever be in that position again." She sniffed, dipping her head to wipe away the tears. "I struggle enough as a covered Muslim woman. I

Open to Love

don't want to have the polygyny fight. I just want one husband who has one family."

"I understand, me too."

"Really? I don't want to force you into anything."

"You're not. I can't think of anything better than making a home and family with you. The contract stays the same. Lunch in the break room?"

"I can eat. *As-salam alaykum.*" Lunch didn't come quick enough.

Wedding Night

"WATCH YOUR STEP, BABE." FAHEEM cast the flashlight from his phone over Hafsah's feet. She took his hand and joined him on the front porch of the large colonial, sitting in the middle of the dark suburban street. "Sorry—" he jingled the keys "—the electrician is coming this week to fix the light. Don't take your shoes off. There are some nails on the floor."

His thumb passed over her hand. Butterflies fluttered at top speed in the base of her stomach. They had started at the wedding and showed no signs of letting up. "That's okay," she giggled, trying to control the cracking in her voice.

"You're shaking." He opened the door and stretched an arm towards the wall. A pendant light filled the entryway, shining on his gorgeous smile. "Are you cold?" He cupped her hands and huffed over them. Any semblance of composure she'd managed to hold onto fell around her feet. She could kick herself for agreeing to see the house first. She wanted him now, but the apartment was so far away.She stepped closer and pinned his gaze. "I'm fine."

"So—" he stroked her cheek "—this is the house." He leaned closer, grazing his full lips against hers. His mustache tickled, sending a charge straight through her. She gave him a light peck then melted against him with a kiss that batted way the butterflies and ushered in hunger for the man who had captured her heart.

Her body shuddered in protest when he tore his soft lips from hers. He backed away, taking her with him. "You can see the rest of the house tomorrow." He flipped a switch next to the wrought iron banister. "There's something I want to show you." They headed up the stairs.

Her heartbeat quickened as they made it to the top. She shouldn't be nervous, but being with Faheem was new. Everything was, and her body was raw with anticipation. The soft glow under the bedroom door invited her to explore whatever her new husband had to offer. He held her hands and pulled her inside. "I wanted our first night together to be in our home—in our bed."

He drew her toward the center of the large room to a canopy bed draped with white sheers and lights strung across and down the posters. "Oh, Faheem. It's beautiful. You did this for me?"

"For us." He reached for the top of her head and pulled at her hijab. It refused to budge. "What's holding this down?"

She laughed, "I got it." She unwrapped the hijab and set it next to flickering flameless candles on the nightstand before taking her braids out of their bun and spreading them across her shoulders. "Better?"

He gasped and ran his fingers through her braids. "You're so beautiful. I didn't even imagine it right." He shrugged out of his shirt.

She traveled her gaze along the trail of hair down his torso. It disappeared into his pants, where a healthy bulge caught her attention. She parted her lips. He claimed them in a hungry kiss. His tongue slid against hers until the entire world melted around them. He unzipped her gown. It fell to the floor along with all meaning save to be with him. His hand smoothed over the spray of goose pimples across her back. "Are you ready?"

They sat on the bed. She laid a hand on his chest. His heartbeat pounded against it, contrasting the serenity she saw on his face. "Yes. Umm, Faheem."

"Mmm?" he moaned while kissing her neck.

"Isn't this your first time?" she asked, becoming increasingly breathless.

"Mmm." He slid his hands down her body and cupped her bottom.

"Aren't you nervous?"

"No," he mumbled between pecks on her shoulder before laying her across the bed. "I'm with you. Besides, like with everything I do—" he stepped out of his pants and laid next to her "—I learned what I needed." The self-assured smirk on his face made her heart dance. He pressed his hard cock against her thigh and glided his fingertips up her side, stopping at her bra. "We're going to do this very well."

Her insides turned to jelly. "Okay."

Faheem murmured a dua before popping open the delicate yellow bra. He brushed his thumb over her nipple until it pebbled. She was magnificent. It was going to be hard to take things slowly. *Don't just jump on her. Let her finish first.* Words from the books he memorized swam in his mind. He put his face over hers, rolling the nipple between his thumb and forefinger. "I want you so much, Hafsah. It feels like I've waited an eternity." He took the other in his mouth. *Don't just jump on her.* His body tingled with desire. *Don't just jump on her.*

He spanned his hand across her stomach and slid it down, slipping under her wet panties, gliding his fingers up and down her firm clit until her arousal moistened them. The feel of her slender fingers wrapping around his stiffness sent jolts of electricity through him. So much to explore. Pushing further into her folds, his head throbbed from senses and reminders spinning like a whirlpool. His cock throbbed with the urge to take her. *Don't just jump on her.* "Please," she groaned, tugging his shoulder.

He peeled the yellow lace panties contrasting her glistening brown skin away and sat on his heels between her legs, stroking her plump, hairless lower lips. "You're so pretty, everywhere." He passed his tongue along his bottom lip and dropped his head between her thighs, licking the soft skin before flicking her inviting clit with his tongue. The room filled with his bride's passion-soaked cries.

Open to Love

He let her hand push him away despite his tongue twitching to go deeper and taste more. He settled between her thighs. She guided his cock into her slick warmth. Each of his long strokes made her wetter. Soon, the sucking sound of their colliding bodies joined her groans. "Hafsah." He swallowed the lump in his throat and upped his cadence. *Let her finish first.*

She dug her fingers into his rump. "Yes, Faheem. Like that. Just like that." Her soft walls tightened around him. *Let her finish first.* Her eyes sparked with lust in the light. She wrapped her thighs around his hips and met his thrusts. The bed shook with his collapsing resistance. He held his breath, trying to prevent going over the edge. *Let her finish first.* He pulled out of her and stilled his aching muscles. His engorged head pulsated in sweet agony between her folds. "What's wrong?"

"Nothing," he rasped, wiping away the sweat stinging his eyes. "I didn't expect it to be so good."

She covered his face with tender kisses. "Neither did I." She pulled him back inside of her and swirled her hips. His entire body prickled. He met her gyrations with increasingly hard thrusts, both panting until his roar of release followed her high-pitched cries of ecstasy.

He fell on top of her, gulping for air until the dizzying excitement from their mutual gratification subsided. *Alhamdulillah.*

"This was so nice," She let out a sultry post-sex sigh. "I'm glad we started here."

"Yeah. This is where we belong. The house will be ready soon enough. Thirsty?" He got off the bed and strutted to the mini-fridge.

She giggled. "Did you think of everything?" She asked, holding up the blankets when he returned.

"Yup." He passed her a bottle of water and crawled underneath. "The kitchen doesn't have a floor yet, so I put snacks up here. I figured we'd work up an appetite."

She cuddled against him. "Indeed, we did."

He settled further into the bed, holding his new wife until sleep overtook them.

* * *

Allahu Akbar, Allahu Akbar.

The sound of Faheem calling the adhan flowed into the bathroom. She squeezed her braids in the towel, then wrapped it around her chest and padded into the room past him. He stood facing the window with his hands cupping his ears and chin lifted. Fajr was always such a peaceful time of the day. It brought a serenity that settled the heart. She picked up her rumpled wedding gown off the floor and shook it out and before smoothing it against her body. There would be extra *dua* to Allah for blessing her with such a great guy.

He hooked an arm around her waist. "As-salam alaykum. You don't need to put that on for salaah." He pressed the small of her back, prodding her forward until they reached one of the doors flanking the bed. He opened it and turned on a light.

Open to Love

   She gasped. Clothes hung at the back of the walk-in closet. "You're amazing." She went inside and picked up a skirt folded on a dresser. "Wait, this is mine."

   "Yeah, your mom snuck a few things out of your place." He opened a drawer, revealing folded rows of bras and panties. "Don't worry, she folded these."

   She hung her arms around his neck. "Look at you, thinking of everything. I never plan for anything. How are you gonna put up with me?"

   He held her hips, flashing a boyish smile. "The way I see it, we complement each other." He covered her mouth. She stepped closer, wiggling her toes against his. He broke the kiss. "Control yourself, Mrs. Qureshi. Save it for after prayer." He patted her on the bottom before making his way into the bedroom.

   She shook her head and held the skirt in front of her. *Alhamdulillah, I have my clothes and man.* After prayer, they went back to bed. She laid her head on his chest and listened to him, describe in detail his plans for their new home.

New Bed

"Okay," Faheem rasped, wiping the sweat from his forehead. "All we have to do is carry it straight into the bedroom." He met Aqil's gaze on the other end of the bulky white mattress. "Got it?"

Aqil's nostrils flared as he bent on his knees, sweat streaming past his thick black eyebrows. "Yeah, man." He heaved and lifted the mattress.

Faheem pulled up his end and walked backward, kicking away a stool next to the kitchen island. It was such a small place, but they could make it work. He carried the mattress into the bedroom. "Put it down here." He dropped it and gulped in the floral air with his hands on his hips. "Thanks, man."

"No problem." Aqil grinned and put his fists on his hips after setting the other end down. "Were taking the old one out now?"

Faheem glanced at the black comforter with huge red roses spread across the bed. The crimson red pillows promised to make a good night's sleep difficult. The bedding matched nothing else in the bedroom, not the blush walls or white contemporary nightstands flanking it. Time to get rid of it. "Yes."

Hafsah glided into the room with two glasses, her black hijab swaying behind her. She stopped in front of him, holding up a glass filled with pale yellow lemonade and ice cubes. "So, you are determined to get my bed out of here?" she asked, giving Aqil the other one.

He put a hand on the new mattress. "This is your bed." He took the glass and a couple of gulps of the sweet drink, gazing over the glass at Hafsah's beautiful face, her brown eyes sparkling. She was sweeter in so many ways but one his tongue longed to taste. Their first time together was amazing, so was every other. He couldn't get enough of her. He passed the glass back. "Now—" he patted her bottom "—If you will excuse us."

Her eyes flashed. The sultry grin that spread across her face sent a charge into his heart that shot lower. "You know that your friend is standing right here, Brother Faheem?"

Aqil yanked at the thick plastic covering the mattress with a small chuckle. "I didn't see anything."

Hafsah giggled and turned. "Let me take the bedding off for you guys." Her round bottom bounced as she bent and jerked the blankets back, inviting him to indulge. He eyed Aqil, who had his back turned to Hafsah and her delightful jiggle. He had to go.

Faheem helped Aqil remove the rest of the plastic before the two of them took the old mattress outside and dropped the new one on top of the box spring. He crossed his arms and surveyed the new bed, his new bed. Now to get his wife on it. "Thanks for helping, man. I can get the boxes myself." He walked into the kitchen.

"Are you sure?" Aqil asked, following. "There are a lot of them."

"I got it." He tossed Aqil a bottle of water and surveyed the great room. Streams of daylight sprayed through it from the windows. Not much room. He'd have to deal with the tiny space until the house was finished.

Hafsah raised from the dark red sofa in the middle of the room. He was really starting to hate the color. She leaned on the island counter, knitting her eyebrows. "You're not staying for lunch, Aqil?"

Aqil put his bottle on the counter and turned it with his fingers. "Umm, I'm not sure."

The doorbell rang. Hafsah said, pushing off the counter. "I am. You're staying."

Faheem propped against the sink and let out a soft huff before taking another swig, watching her walk away. Alone time would have to wait.

"As-salam alaykum." Tarika's voice shot into the apartment. "I hope you guys are ready to indulge." She waltzed with a hand on one hip and holding up a pie pan in the other. "I have the best stuff imaginable." Her bright smile didn't fade when she faced Aqil and him on the other side of the counter.

"Wa alaykum salam, sister." Aqil picked up the water bottle and began to screw the cap back and forth, biting the bottom of his smiling lip. "It's good to see you."

Faheem shook his head. Great, he now had two cockblockers. "Wa alaykum salam, Tarika. Jazakallah for bringing it. What kind is it?" He caught Hafsah's gaze, an amused expression on her face.

"Sweet potato," Tarika said, setting the plastic-covered pie down and inhaling. "Mashallah, Hafsah. It smells good. What did you make?"

"Lamb chops." Hafsah graced the seat next to her. "I figured Faheem and Aqil would want a good meal after moving everything. Your pie is just what we needed."

"Yeah." Faheem shot past the counter. His growling stomach at that smell of garlic and lamb provided the final wrench in his plans to taste more of Hafsah. "Come on, Aqil, let's start bringing in the boxes." Might as well do some work and have food. He headed out the door, not waiting for a response from anyone. He reached over the truck's tailgate and pulled out a big brown box. He turned and shoved it at Aqil's chest.

"Yo, man," Aqil grunted and teetered, wrapping his arms around the brown cardboard. "What's your problem?"

"You—" he leaned over the box, pointing to the apartment door "— Tarika."

Open to Love

Aqil's eyes widened before he threw his head back, laughing. "Ah, man, I'm sorry. I didn't mean to...how about I just tell Hafsah that I have to go?"

"No, she made food for you." He grabbed another box. "You can't leave. Stay." He hefted the box on his chest, huffing in the stale parking lot air as he walked up the concrete walkway. "But eat fast."

***

Hafsah pulled Tarika into her arms. "Jazakallah, girl." She hugged her best friend, the faint smell of coconut oil drifting from under her hijab. "It was so great having you here."

"Mmm." Tarika patted her back. "Although, I think Faheem wasn't all that thrilled. He was pretty much pouting all through dinner." She stepped back onto the front stoop, her round cheeks shone under the light overhead. She was so beautiful and such a good friend. "And the way he looked at you across the table, I think he wanted to be alone with his wife."

Hafsah pulled the top of her draped hijab forward and tucked some stray coils underneath it. "Yeah, but I think he had a good time. Aqil is a nice guy."

"He's all right but very quiet. He hardly said ten words during dinner. Anyway, I think Faheem would've had a better time if we weren't here." Tarika snickered. "I'll call you tomorrow." She turned and walked down the path, lined with mown grass. "As-salam alaykum."

"Wa alaykum salam." Hafsah waved and watched her get into the small red car before closing and locking the front door. She turned the lights off, dimming the now quiet apartment. The faint scent of lamb and cozy vibes from hours of laughter wrapped around her and nestled into her heart. Dinner with friends was something new. Life with Faheem always seemed to have a new and wonderful thing just ahead. She put the last of the dishes in the washer and pushed the on switch. Padding into the bedroom, she zipped open the large bag of new bedding in the middle of the bed while a faint hum of streaming shower water filtered into the bedroom. She flipped open the blush comforter and pillowcases, draping them over the lower half of the bed. They complimented the room perfectly like he did her.

The bathroom door opened just when she finished tucking in the last corner of the fitted sheet. "There are new pillows too." Faheem strutted out in a towel, beads of water hanging from the ends of his hair and streaming between the curly hairs of his pecs. He stopped in front of her. The fresh scent of his moist skin beckoned her to touch it, but he made the first move, cupping her chin and stroking her jaw with his fingertips. The soft-touch sent electric warmth through her. "I hope you understand why I wanted a new bed. I won't tolerate the memory of another man lingering around me as I lay with my wife."

She looked into his smoldering eyes and swallowed. "I get it." She stepped closer and hooked the top of his towel with her forefinger. "Should I get rid of the towels too?" She looked down at the small bulge in the front of it. She tugged. A warm prickle sprung between her legs as the soft burgundy terry cloth loosened around his waist.

He clasped her hand and the towel. "No." he brushed his lips against hers, nibbling her bottom lip. "I want to see you first." He sat on the edge of the bed, leaning on his elbows. The towel fell open. One muscular thigh swayed back and forth. "Take all of that off. It's for other people. Not me."

She felt a tingle spray up her arms at his command. He was not playing. She trailed her gaze up his body, meeting his as she unpinned her hijab and let it fall around her feet. "You want to see all of me, Faheem?"

"You're wasting time. I've waited long enough. Get those damn clothes off," He cupped his stiff cock over the towel, "and get on this."

Her heart raced as she squirmed out of her black overgarment and tank top before yanking her floral leggings and panties down her thighs. She panted, aching to start the ride he offered. He had dissolved all her anxieties about being with a virgin. He wasn't timid and awkward—far from it. His sensual confidence had her reeling from his explorations and the new experiences he gave her. She stepped closer and yanked back the towel. His stiffness jerked. She gasped as her folds moistened. He turned her on like a switch sometimes.

She lowered to her knees and glided her fingertips up the warm shaft skin. Its silkiness sent a quiver to her lips. She whispered a dua before brushing them against it. His scent and heavy breathing fogged her head into an erotic lightheadedness. "Hafs—" His legs shook on either side of her waist. She made tiny licks all the way up to the tip and slid her tongue under the head. He wanted her to get on it, and she was about to do just that. She filled her mouth with his hard cock, sliding her head up and down, gagging just a little, hot convulsions of desire running through her each time it poked the back of her throat. It all felt so good. He grabbed the hair at the back of her head. "Okay," he heaved, "you have to stop before it's all over."

She tilted her head, grinning at his glistening face. "Now what, brother?"

He chuckled and guided her over him and up his body. She started to settle her hips on his, but he grasped them and pulled her higher. "Wha—what are you doing?" His smile disappeared between her thighs. She threw her head back. His tongue flicked and circled her clit. He rolled his head, and her entire world spun. "Oh." She fell forward on her hands and clenched the new sheet. He smacked her bottom. Her body shuddered, and folds burned hot to the point of totally consuming her and bringing everything around them to ashes. "Wait, Faheem. I'm gonna come." He moaned, grabbing her butt cheeks and pushing his tongue further into her. She cried out, tumbling over the edge of sensual frenzy, his tongue licking her flowing juices.

She fell on the bed, her insides still in the throes of satisfaction. Faheem lay on top of her, placing the tip of his cock between her bottom lips. "See," he said, his breath briny, "you could've had me eating you earlier instead of feeding everybody."

She laughed. "Lesson learned." She pulled his lips to hers, his moist beard tickling her chin. "No more dinner guests until we move."

"Good. Now—" he filled her with his throbbing cock "—it's my turn." He moved slowly in and out of her tender walls.

As the light stinging from her orgasm faded, a renewed warmth began to spread. She entwined their legs and dug into his sweaty buttocks. He squeezed her, going faster. "Yes, give it to me, Faheem." He interrupted his fixed stride with hard thrusts. She braced on her heels and met him until their hips became one. His roar of release burst into her ear. She caught her breath with his satiated body splayed over her.

"Wow." He gulped. "Is it always going to be like this?"

"We can try to make sure it is." She kissed down his cheek, settling a long kiss on his mouth, the smell and taste of her lingered on them. He was magnificent.

He pulled from her and wrapped the towels back around his waist. "I like that idea." He left the room and brought back a shopping bag with pillows bursting from the top. He finished putting on the pillows and blankets while she freshened up in the bathroom. She pulled up striped pajama bottoms around her hips and tugged on a red camisole from the drawer. He yanked off the tape from the top of a box with a loud rip and started taking out clothes, stopping at a pair of grey sweats. "Let's get to bed…well…sleep." He settled between the sheets. "Come here."

She cuddled under his arm and laid her head on his chest, fingering the hairs. "See," she sighed, "not so bad being here, right?"

"I guess," he mumbled, stroking her shoulder.

She looked up. "It'll be okay. I can make you happy here."

The wrinkle between his brow softened. "You can make me happy anywhere."

Tell Him

Hafsah unpinned her hijab and let it fall around her shoulders. She closed her eyes and rubbed the back of her neck, enjoying the cool air on it. There was so much to say today. Where to begin?

"So," Dr. Rahman patted the large puff at the back of her head and clicked the pin in her hand, "It's been a few weeks since we had a chance to talk. What's been going on in your life? How are you adjusting to living with Faheem?" She crossed her legs and leaned forward, spreading her full brown lips into a smile that immediately set Hafsah at ease.

She sunk deeper into her chair. Dr. Rahman always made her feel like her concerns were the most important in the world. Their sessions helped her survive Mahmoud's messiness and heal enough to accept the love Faheem had for her. "Alhamdulillah. Things are good. I need to get used to having a husband who comes home every night."

"Hard adjustment?"

"A little bit. I mean, Faheem is great, but I felt a little suffocated at first. We worked together.

We went home together. I didn't have any space. Things are a little better now that I'm not working. I get to be alone."

Dr. Rahman raised her eyebrows and tapped the pen on her pad. "You mentioned in our last session that you were thinking about quitting. It must've taken a lot of trust, considering your experience with your first husband."

"Yeah. Faheem is different. I can't guarantee he won't hurt me, but he isn't as controlling as Mahmoud."

"How does that make you feel?"

"Good. Scared. I don't know. He's too perfect, you know?" She sighed and leaned her head on the back of the chair. "The worse he does is sometimes, he gets really quiet, and I don't know what he's thinking. I have to sit and wait for him to open up. It's infuriating, but then he smiles, and I turn to mush. I can't stay mad at him."

Dr. Rahman chuckled. "The first year of marriage requires a lot of work getting to know each other and learning how to communicate. Things should get calmer."

"Not any time soon."

"Why not?"

"I'm pregnant."

"Hmm—" Dr. Rahman nodded. "Okay."

"Exactly." She sat straight. "Everything is happening so fast. We didn't try not to get pregnant, but I never thought it would happen so quickly. From the moment he asked me to marry him, our life has been running at top speed."

"That's not necessarily a bad thing."

"Maybe, but I never get a chance to breathe or settle."

"Do you want the baby?"

"Absolutely. I've wanted to be a mother for a while. It's one of the reasons why my last marriage ended."

"Have you told Faheem?"

"No. I took the test after he left for work this morning."

"Do you think he doesn't want the baby?"

"He said he wants kids, but already?"

"Well, he's married to you and has been having unprotected sex with you. He must know pregnancy is a possibility. You've told me that you love and trust him. He makes you feel safe and loved. Why not tell him that he's going to be a father?"

She sighed and passed a hand over her queasy stomach. Wife and mother in less than six months. All the blessings raining down overwhelmed her, but Allah was merciful. "You're right. I'll tell him tonight."

After her session with Dr. Rahman ended, Hafsah donned her hijab and hopped into the car. She merged into traffic, passing shopping centers and patches of forest. As she made her way down the highway, countless ways she could tell Faheem about the baby swirled in her mind. Any fears that he didn't want the baby were irrational, yet here she was, fluttering heart and all. She flexed her fingers on the steering wheel and let her shoulder drop. *What an idiot, getting stuck thinking something bad is going to happen when you know deep down it won't.* She needed to make a major mind shift.

She parked the car and grabbed a cart from in front of the halal meat store. Her stomach turned from the blast of smells as she walked through automatic doors. Spices to the right, a case of food in warmers to the left. It all smacked her in the face. *Stop being such a god damn wimp and get dinner.* She also had to grow a pair about Faheem.

She made her way to the glass case, grinning back at the short, slender Desi man wearing a white apron covered in blood. "As-salam alaykum, sister. What can I get you?"

"Wa alaykum salam. Can I get two chicken breasts?"

Sketchpad

Hafsah yawned and stretched, lifting her heavy lids. The sounds of pots and pans clanking floated into the bedroom with crackling and sizzling. She swung her feet over the edge of the bed, holding her growling stomach. Alhamdulillah, someone was cooking. She rubbed an achy eyelid as she shuffled into the great room in her bare feet. Faheem pushed a spatula around a smoking pan on the stove. He paused and pushed his rolled dress shirt sleeves further up his arms then raised a pot lid. He coughed as a bloom of steam burst in his face. She giggled. He looked so adorable when he was being domestic. "As-salam alaykum." She yawned and rounded the kitchen counter.

"When did you get home?" She wrapped her arms around his waist and spied the dim sky outside the window.

"Wa alaykum salam. A while ago." He turned off the stove. "Are you hungry?"

"I'm sorry. I meant to cook, but the trip to Dr. Rahman's office left me beat."

"It's fine." He turned, his eyes sparkling, forehead coated with beads of sweat. "I know you've been tired lately."

"Yeah, but you've been working all day. I could at least have a hot meal for you."

He shook his head and gave her a few pecks on her lips that made her insides tingle—a welcome departure from the achiness that had overtaken her the past couple of weeks. "How many times do I have to tell you that I'm not one of those men who stomp around demanding his wife do all of the housework? You take care of me. I take care of you. That's the deal. Plates, please."

She opened a cabinet and took out two black square plates. "I know, but I'm home all day now."

"Yes, exactly where we both want you to be," he said, putting yellow rice with bursts of red tomato and green peppers on each plate. "I live here too. What kind of partner would I be if I didn't help?" He took the plates and walked around the counter. "Can you bring the chicken?"

She picked up the glass baking dish, stretching her arms to keep the garlic smell drifting from the two pieces of chicken breast inside as far away from her nose as possible. Too late. She swallowed the queasy feeling as she followed him. Lumbering to the table, she sat and braced her forehead in her hand, taking a few deep breaths until the dizziness faded.

"I guess you're not in the mood for chicken. You all right?" Faheem leaned over her, rubbing her

Open to Love

back. She lifted her head. The concern on his face added guilt to the nausea. She had to tell him.

"I'm fine. I guess not."

"I can make you something else. What would you like?"

To throw all this stuff out the window. "Nothing. The rice is fine. You've done too much already." She lifted the fork. Rice couldn't be bad. Oh, yes, it could. The scent of green peppers triggered her stomach into a worse episode. She started to make a mental list of things to put right in the trash ASAP. Those were at the top.

"This?" He sat next to her. "It wasn't hard. The Prophet did stuff around the house, and so can I. Besides—" he slid his chair closer and patted her stomach "—you're going to need all the help you can get with a baby coming."

Her fork landed on the plate with a clatter. She met his gaze. The knowing smirk on his face overpowered the morning sickness. "How did you know?"

He chuckled and held her face between his hands. "I'm an observant man, Hafsah." He kissed her and picked up her plate of rice. "You've been sleeping a lot and sick all the time." He walked into the kitchen. She turned in her chair, staring at his swagger. "Also—" he stopped in front of a cabinet "—we haven't had any interruptions in the bedroom, which I've got to admit has been nice." He ripped open a pack of saltines and set them in front of her. "It doesn't take a genius."

She took a square white cracker from the sleeve and fiddled it between her fingers. "You're okay with me being pregnant?"

He dropped a piece of chicken on his rice and put the baking dish on the counter. "Of course. I'm the one who got you pregnant, remember." He cut through the meat and shoved a chunk in his mouth, chewing with a smug grin.

"Yes, but you don't think it's too soon? It doesn't seem like everything is happening fast?"

"Nope," he mumbled and swallowed with a twinkle in his eyes. "It's happening according to Allah's plan. You can't be that far along, so the house will be finished before the baby is born, inshallah." He looked down at her hands. "Are you okay with having a baby?"

She followed his gaze. The cracker was a pile of crumbs on the table. "Oh, yes. I'm happy. I was just worried about what you thought." She shoved a new cracker into her mouth.

"I think it's amazing." He reached for her hands. She loved him. Of that, he was sure, but she still didn't fully trust in what they had. "You're my wife, having my baby. We're a family. I need you to believe in us. Believe in me and my ability to be a husband and father. I'm ready for all of it."

She lifted and kissed his hands. "I do believe in you, Faheem. You're smart and loving and caring, everything I've always wanted."

"I better be." He winked and pressed his lips against hers.

Open to Love

She turned her head. "Sorry," she said, closing her eyes. "Your breath...that chicken...I can't."

He fell back in his chair, laughing. "Eat your crackers, woman." After dinner and salaah, he put leftovers in a container for work and cleaned the kitchen. By the time he came back from taking the trash to the dumpster, Hafsah was curled in a ball on the sofa. "Come on, Babe. Let's go to bed." He guided her into the bedroom, returning to the living room once he had her settled between the blankets. He unfastened the buckles of his brown leather messenger bag, taking out the matching portfolio and a pen. He flopped on the sofa and flipped through the lined yellow pad, stopping at a clean page and writing the word *nursery* at the top. He tapped the pen on the pad until a steady beat echoed through the great room. Confirmation of his suspicions that Hafsah was pregnant sent him reeling, but he couldn't let her know that. He was the rock of the family, their family.

He doodled a square. The small room next to the master would be perfect. He etched a doorway symbol on the imagined wall the rooms shared. The house renovations had changed from the moment Hafsah took ownership of his heart. Her happiness became the most important thing to him, and he was determined to give mommy and baby everything they needed.

He wrote lists of modifications, contractors and suppliers. Only the best for the new Qureshi. He smiled and let out a chuckle. He was going to be a dad. He stopped the pen mid-word and looked up.

Lyndell Williams

The quiet dimness did nothing to ebb his dislike for the apartment.

"Faheem?" Hafsah's soft moan drifted into his thoughts.

He closed the portfolio and dropped it on the sofa. "Coming." He turned off the light and padded into the bedroom. "I've gotta get us out of here."

***

Hafsah filled the white mug with the pictures of blueprints on either side. She sipped the light-yellow ginger-lemon tea. It eased her queasy stomach while she swiped through the paint color pallets on the tablet screen. *Subhanallah.* There were so many. How did he expect her to decide?

Faheem had thrown his toolbelt over his shoulder and left to work on the house after Fajr prayer, giving her strict instructions to make all nursery decorating choices. She looked out the kitchen window at the dimming sky. She had put it off all day. Hubby was going to be home soon. She took the tablet with her and set it next to the stove, swallowing back the threatening nausea from the pungent bloom of steam wafting in her face. She scanned the pastels on the screen while stirring the bubbling contents inside the pot. Faheem would be exhausted when he got home. A nice meal was mandatory.

Her heart soared at the sound of keys jiggling in the front door lock tumblers. As usual, he was early or on time. "As-salam alaykum," she sang, lowering the lid on the pot. "I didn't hear the truck." She turned, arms aching to wrap around her husband. "I guess I was too busy concentrating on—" She clenched the wooden spoon and glared, bile bubbling up her throat. "What the hell are you doing here?"

"Salams, Habibti," Mahmoud said, smirking as he ambled toward her.

New Things

MAHMOUD WALKED AROUND THE boxes stacked near the doorway. "That's not a very warm welcome."

"It wasn't meant to be," Hafsah snapped. "Stay away from me." Of course, the jackass didn't listen, moving closer. She backed away. Her backside hit the stove. The pot lid rattled. She sucked air through her teeth, rubbing where she had been burned.

He smiled, gazing down at her cleavage. "Didn't you miss me? I sure missed you."

"I asked what're you doing here? You know what?" She pushed past him. "Get out." It must be a dream. She hit her head while looking at dull paint samples and slipped into a coma. *What a fucking mess.* She snatched a hijab from the hook next to the door.

"I'm not leaving until you listen to me." He took her hand and pressed it to his lips. "I know you're mad, but you can't deny how good we were together." He must have lost his mind? She snatched her hand away and scoffed. "You are a real piece of work." She stood in the open doorway. "I don't need to listen to anything you have to say."

"Why do you have to make things difficult? You're going want to hear this." He leaned closer, his lips in a small pout. "Afaf dead."

She stopped wrapping the hijab around her head and met his downcast gaze. "Afaf is what?"

"Dead. A car accident two months ago."

She cleared her throat and muttered a dua, breathing back the guilt welling in her gut. She had imagined Afaf disappearing so many times before, not dead, just gone. "I'm sorry for your loss."

He sighed. "Yeah. It's been hard. Our daughter is living with her parents. I've been lonely." Her arm prickled where his fingers glided down it. "Then I realized that it's not a total loss. I still have you."

She raised her eyebrows. "You have who?"

"You." Afaf was a good wife, but she never was you. I had to marry her. I chose to marry you. Now, we can be together."

She took a step back, tripping onto the stoop. Did he really think that he could just plop her into Afaf's place like they were interchangeable? He was definitely out of his mind. She tightened the hijab around her face. "I'm not doing this with you, Mahmoud." She scanned the parking lot. *I don't believe this. I have to get rid of him before Faheem comes home.* She pulled the long fabric down her bare arms. "Listen," she seethed, pointing a finger at him. "You don't have a chance in hell of getting me back. That's not happening. Get it through your thick, arrogant skull. I'm not in love with you anymore."

He stood in front of her, pulling up one corner of his mouth. "You don't mean that."

She sniggered in his smug face. "Oh, trust me. I mean it. I don't want you. Now, give me my key and get out of here before my husband comes home."

He scowled, his eyes narrowing. "Your what?"

She lifted her chin and gloated at his shock. He was clearly under the delusion that having sex with her meant she was his forever. "My husband."

"Who would marry you? You're old and divorced."

She pressed her lips and shook her head. Words like that stung in the past, made her think she was not worthy and lucky to be with someone like him. Not anymore. "You did, and you're standing here, all desperate to get back with me. Sucks for you."

"You were always ungrateful. I took you when nobody else wanted you."

She folded her arms and balanced on one leg. "Well, someone else wants me, and he'll be home any minute."

He pointed in her face. "You listen—"

A roaring engine echoed between the rows of buildings, kicking up her heart a notch. Faheem's large black pickup truck turned into the stall and came to a screeching halt. She shielded her eyes from the burning pain of the bright lights flooding the porch. Every nerve fired through her. "Damn."

The headlights went black. The door swung open, hitting the car next to it.

She saw Faheem jump out and reach into the back of the truck. After a large clank, He stormed towards them, holding a crowbar with a hooked end and pointing. "Who the hell is this?"

She dashed down the walkway, her bare feet slapping against the concrete. "As-salam alaykum. It's okay, Faheem. He's leaving." He stomped on the curb, saying nothing. His arm snaked around her waist. She hugged his shoulders. The safety of being in his arms didn't help slow her racing heart. The parking lot light shone on his tight jaw and flared nostrils, his grip crushing her against him. Angry Faheem was scary as hell.

He practically dragged her back up the walkway, stopping in front of Mahmoud. She watched Faheem size him up. "Well?"

Mahmoud crossed his arms and stared down his nose. "I'm the ex."

"What do you want?"

"I came to talk to my—to Hafsah."

Faheem tightened his hand around the crowbar. *So, this motherfucker wants to go there?* His nerves had sprung with rage when he turned into the parking lot and saw his wife standing in her nightgown, arguing with some random guy. So, this was Mahmoud? Once weary, every muscle aching from a long day of putting down floors now twitched with an urge to punch the cocky smile off his face. He was going to set the man who put his

Open to Love

finger in Hafsah's face straight, but first, he had to get her somewhere safe just in case things got ugly.

He looked at her. "How are you feeling?"

Her eyes met his, glistening with tears. "I'm good," she stammered through her quivering lips. His heart wrenched from seeing her so upset, but soothing her fears would have to wait until later.

Making sure to keep his tone even despite the tornado of emotions spinning inside of him, he let her go and spread a hand across her lower abdomen. "No morning sickness?" He watched Mahmoud's self-assured grin disappear. The corners of his mouth twitched. *That's right. I hit it, and I put it to work.*

"A little, but the tea you left helped."

He took her hand. "Alhamdulillah, dinner ready?" he asked while leading her to the porch. "Can you get it on the table? I'm starving."

"Sure, but Faheem—"

"Jazakallah." He patted her bottom and closed the door once she was inside. He filled his chest, striding back down the walkway until he faced Mahmoud. Breathing in a mixture of car exhaust fumes and tension hanging between them under the streetlight, he kept his body rigid as he stared at the man who stepped into his life, primed to destroy his happiness. The possibility that he would have to send Mahmoud to the hospital was an acceptable one. He had taken down bigger and badder for far less. "My wife has dinner waiting, so I'm going to keep this brief."

"Yeah, alright." Mahmoud chuckled and squared his shoulders back. "You're kinda young. What did she do, pick you up from the nearest high school?"

He stepped closer. "There's nothing and no one for you here. Come around Hafsah again, and you're gonna have a serious problem. As-salam alaykum." This was going to be the last time this man came sniffing around his wife.

Mahmoud slowly blinked, turning his head from side to side. People stood in their doorways and in the parking lot. "Wa alaykum salam," he said, backing away.

Faheem didn't let his hands relax until he saw Mahmoud get into a car and pull out of the complex. He went into the house. Once inside, he scanned the great room. "Hafsah?"

"I'm in the kitchen." She rounded the counter, balancing a large bowl. "Dinner is ready." She set it on the table and wiped the tears from her cheek. "Faheem. I know how it must've looked, but I can explain."

"There's nothing to explain." He kicked off his work boots and closed the distance between them. Holding her in his arms, he buried his fingers in her soft coils and claimed her mouth in a kiss until her tense body softened against him. He met her gaze. "I'm going to wash up." In the bathroom, he clenched the marble vanity and took deep breaths until his racing heart calmed. Warm water from a quick shower helped soothe the tense muscles. He

Open to Love

had done what he needed to protect his wife and unborn child—his family.

He pulled a tank tee shirt down his torso as he padded to the table. "Mashallah, this looks delicious, Babe." He sat and piled his plate high. Although he no longer felt the same tensions as earlier, the unusual silence kept peace at bay. Hafsah stabbed at her food. She looked everywhere except his direction. "Did you pick a paint color?"

"No." He peaked under the table. Her legs shook over her curled toes.

He reached across the table. "Come here."

He settled her onto his lap and laid her head on his shoulder. "Faheem, I didn't ask Mahmoud to come here. He just showed up."

"I know." He stroked her back, enjoying the scent of her hair tickling his nose. "My father told me the day before the wedding to watch out for your ex-husband. He said, 'Hafsah is a good woman. He's going to realize what he gave up.' I guess he did, but that's too bad for him. You're mine now, and I won't be stupid enough to let you go."

She ran her fingers over his beard. "I'm not letting you go either. I love you. I wouldn't do anything to jeopardize what we have."

"Of course not. Remember when I told you that you had to start trusting me?"

She lifted her head. "Yes, and I do."

"I trust you too, Hafsah, with everything but choosing a paint color."

She laughed and got up. "I'll get the tablet."

He resumed eating. "By the way," he said between bites, "I'm gonna take the next few weeks off. I want to get the house ready enough so that we can move in by the end of the month."

"I can't think of anything better." She bent over him and covered his lips. It was his toes' turn to curl. She had become his everything so quickly. He would have to hit the ground running in the morning.

Ibrahim Qureshi

6 Months Later

"Okay, Little Man—" Faheem carried the car seat inside and set it on the floor next to the staircase. "—you're home with Mommy and Daddy." He greeted the house and looked inside at their newborn son. The car seat headrest framed his brown face, a tiny version of Hafsah's except for the eyes. Those came from daddy. He turned to see Hafsah come through the door beaming. She looked nothing like a woman who went through hours of grueling labor just a few days before. He dropped the diaper bag and opened his arms. "Come here."

"My pleasure." She smiled, wrapping her arms around his waist and looking up with puckered lips. He obeyed their command and pressed his lips to hers. He slid a hand down her back and settled it on her round bottom, a little thicker from motherhood. He had sorely felt her absence from their bed while she was in the hospital. "Nice," she said after breaking their kiss, "but are you trying to start on the next baby already? I do have a waiting period." She pushed against his chest.

He groaned and let his arms fall. "Don't remind me."

She shook her head and walked around him. "You're pathetic. Forty days isn't that long."

He spun and held her from behind, pressing his cheeks to hers. "It's an eternity. You know how much I love being with you. The next month and a half will be torture." He looked down at Ibrahim. "He's worth it, though."

She giggled. "Yeah. He's worth it all." He rocked her in his arms as they stood over the baby. Ibrahim's little mouth opened, letting out small gurgles. "Uh-oh—" Hafsah put her hand to her breasts "—somebody is ready to eat."

"Already? You just fed him before leaving the hospital."

She bent down toward the car seat. "That's newborns."

He moved her hand away. "No, I got him. Where do you want me to bring him?"

"Upstairs—" she unpinned her hijab and draped it over the iron banister "—to the nursery, please. I'll change and feed him."

He picked up the car seat and climbed the stairs, glancing back. "How about I change him, and you can get into some pajamas? The doctor said to rest."

"That sounds good." She stifled a yawn with the back of her hand. "Jazakallah."

Open to Love

"You can finally relax in the finished house." He continued to the nursery with her following.

"Yeah, right. I still have to finish the unpacking I was doing when my water broke."

"That's been handled." He set the car seat in the middle of the round shag area rug in the middle of the room and unbuckled the latches, lifting Ibrahim's tiny body. He was so light. "Tarika, Ma, and your mother came and put away everything, and Aqil and I cleared the boxes."

"Alhamdulillah." She tilted her head and reached for Ibrahim. "Are you sure you can handle changing him."

He put the baby against his chest and lifted his chin. "How dare you doubt my ability to care for my son." They laughed. "Go, change. I got him." Hafsah disappeared around the doorway. Ibrahim, as if knowing his food source just left, began to fuss. "It's all right, Little Man. Mommy will be back." He laid his son on the mahogany changing table and got to work. He had him changed and dressed when he heard Hafsah.

"Faheem, can you bring the baby here?"

"Sure thing. Let's go see what Mommy needs."

Hafsah lay under the blankets, yawning and tying a satin print headscarf on her head. "I'm sorry. I am more tired than I thought. I'll feed him here." She pulled up her pajama tee.

"No problem. Do you want some water or something?" He put Ibrahim in her arms. His heart skipped as he watched her lay down with him and stroke his head as she nursed.

"Water, please."

"You got it." He flew down the stairs and past the pillars into the kitchen. His phone rang. Hafsah's mother's name shone on the screen. He took a water bottle from the fridge and answered. "As-salam alaykum, Ma."

"*Wa alaykum salam. Hafsah and Ibrahim settled?*"

"Yes. She's in the bed with him."

"*Good. Now, remember, don't let her do anything but take care of herself and that baby.*"

"I remember, Ma." He went back up the stairs. "I hired a cleaning person, and the freezer is full of food from you, Tarika and Mom. We're set." Sounds from Ibrahim suckling greeted him when he got back to the room. Hafsah was fast asleep on her side with him pressed next to her. "I gotta go, Ma." He whispered as he approached the bed. "I'll call you later. As-salam alaykum." He put the water bottle down and lay on the other side of his wife, laying an arm across both and burying his nose in her scarf. Domestic bliss attained. They were a solid family that no one could shake apart.

Open to Love

Glossary of Islamic Terms

Allah- God
Allahu Akbar- God is the greatest.
Al hamdulillah- The praise is for Allah.
As-salamu alaykum- Peace upon you. It is a greeting used by Muslims when they meet each other anywhere.
Bismillah- In the name of Allah or with the name of Allah.
dua- Supplication to AllahFajr
Fajr- Early morning prayer before sunrise
ghusl- A full bath performed for purification after sexual relations or after menses.
halal- Something permissible
haram- Something impermissible
hijab- A scarf used by Muslim women that covers the hair, ears, neck, and the breast area.iddah
Inshaa-llah- If it is Allah's will
Jazakallah – May Allah reward you.
Mashallah – It is as Allah wills
salaah - prayer
Subhanallah- Glory to Allah
talaq- Divorce
Wa-alaykumu salam - It is the response to someone greeting a person and means 'and may peace be upon you.'

wali- A male representative for a woman to get married. It is usually a male relative. If there is no Muslim male relative then she is appointed a wali from the community.

Open to Love

Acknowledgements

Alhamdulillah, I've been blessed by the Creator with a great bunch of people.

A warm thank to Sandra Barkevich for being a patient friend and writing coach. I couldn't have even imagined writing this novel without her gentle guidance, encouragement and support.

I have to thank my girls–Djamila Abdel-Jaleel, Nadia Anwar, Maritza Flowers as well as my beautiful and talented daughter Hameedah Poulos for listening to me day and night—night and day—and day and night again—as I worked and flustered over finishing this book.

Jazakallah to my wonderful husband, who works incredibly hard so I can do what I love and stays blissfully ignorant about just how much heat I stoke.

THANKS FOR READING!

I hope you enjoyed Hafsah and Faheem's story of love and perseverance. Please leave a review on Amazon and Goodreads so I can continue to bring readers stories!

CONTACT ME

I would love to hear from you.
Email - laylafied@gmail.com
Website - www.laylawriteslove.com

FOLLOW ME

Facebook - https://www.facebook.com/laylawriteslove/
Instagram - https://www.instagram.com/laylawriteslove/
Twitter - https://twitter.com/laylawriteslove
Amazon - https://amazon.com/author/laylawriteslove

Bonus Reads

Enjoy these sweet romance short stories from my Layla Writes Love blog and published anthologies. In addition, I have included the first chapters of books one and two of the steamy and exciting Brothers in Law Series.

TURNING AROUND

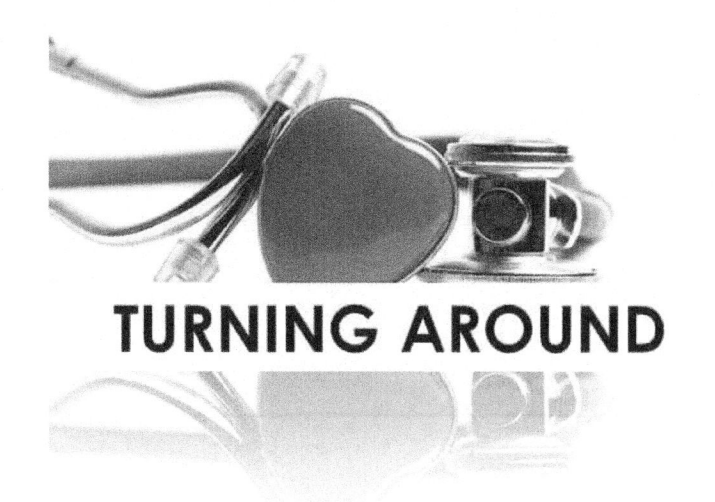

LYNDELL WILLIAMS

Turning Around

Justin unwrapped his throbbing hand and peered at the puncture through his palm, still oozing blood. He slammed his angular eyes shut and winced. "He's so fired." People with various injuries and illnesses stuffed the room, but it was the statuesque woman standing at the desk who struck him. Tension covered her face but did not detract from her beauty. He was so awestruck that the stabbing pain all but disappeared. She took some papers from the nurse, turned and batted thick lashes over her glistening oval eyes while she scanned the room. She held her full brown bottom lip between white teeth and stroked the back of the little boy hugging her leg.

"Excuse me." Justin struggled to keep the blood-soaked towel in place while he stood. He flashed a comforting grin. "You can have this seat." It was as if all the surrounding people disappeared when their gazes met.

Her brown cheeks grew into kissable orbs, flanking her bright smile. "Oh, thank you." She whisked the boy onto a voluptuous hip and meandered through the crowd, stopping just in front of him. Her smile faded as she took in his frame and stared at the crimson-stained towel. "No, I can't take your seat." She hiked the little boy further up her hip. He moaned; her black coils covered the top of his head as he nuzzled his caretaker's slender brown neck. "You're hurt."

"What, this," Justin lifted his arm and chuckled to mask the pain shooting through it, "it's nothing, really. Please, sit."

"Thanks." She settled into the seat between a lady holding a crying baby and a man whose sobriety was highly questionable. Her lovely face disappeared as she dipped her head and wiped at the jaw of the little boy.

Justin found an empty spot on the opposite wall, leaned, and waited for someone to bellow his name. Although the woman's attention obviously focused on her charge, Justin kept glancing in her direction. When the man seated next to her staggered up and wobbled towards the shouting nurse, he practically dove to fill the newly vacant chair. Not the smoothest move, but necessary to ensure he got to sit next to her. Another smile was his reward. He was sure the heat rushing up his face was reddening his light tan skin.

"So, what happened?" She cast Justin a quizzical look and rocked the little boy.

"I had a new worker today who got a little too excited with a nail gun." Justin leaned his arm on the back of the chair. "I'll definitely be handing him a pink slip."

"I bet." Her endearing giggle made his heart skip a beat. "What do you do?"

"I own a construction business." He tilted his head. "What about little man, here? He's sick?"

"Yeah." She brushed her lips against the small forehead. "I think it's an ear infection."

Turning Around

"Justin," his name wafted through the air, "Justin Lang?"

He set his jaw. *Perfect timing.* "Here." He rose and looked down at the nameless beauty. "Nice meeting you, ummm—"

"Monique," she slowly blinked and smiled, "and this is Jamal."

"Nice to meet you both. I'm Justin."

Monique laughed. "I kinda heard. Feel better, Justin."

A knot of regret twisted in his gut as he got further away from Monique and closer to the nurse. A nagging surged through his mind not to let this be the last time he saw her. "Just give me a second." Justin filled his lungs and spun in his work boots, turning away from the irritated nurse. "Right." He closed the distance between them and smiled down at Monique's surprised face. "I'm sorry. I can't walk through those doors without knowing I at least took a shot at getting to know you." Justin reclaimed the empty seat. "I hope you don't think I'm creepy or have a jealous boyfriend or husband about to come through those doors to knock me out, but can you just take my number?" He patted his t-shirt and pants pockets. "Then you can call me, if you want. I hope you do 'cause I can't wait to learn all I can about you."

Monique squinted. "Are you hitting on me in an emergency room?"

Justin rubbed the bundle of muscles at the base of his neck. "Yeah and looking like something from a horror movie while I do." Their shared laugh eased his frazzled nerves. Maybe he had a chance in hell.

"Don't worry, there's no boyfriend or husband ready to plaster you. It's just me and Jamal." She took a deep breath, smirked and reached into her purse. "Give me your number and go before you bleed to death or somethin'"

***

Justin turned off the Harley's roaring engine and popped the kickstand. He whipped off his helmet and glanced at the black Mustang parked next to him in the double driveway. A surge of excitement shot through him. His beloved was home. The walkway leading to the brick single-family detached house on the quiet suburban street seemed endless. Monique had only been away on business for a week, but it felt like forever. Taking care of Jamal and accepting extra clients helped pass the time while she was gone, but the longing gnawing at him while he laid alone on their new bed in the house he built for them made their time apart unbearable.

He cleared the porch and grunted as he assaulted the doorknob with his keys. "Come on." He threw the mahogany door open. "Babe?" His voice echoed through the open-concept first floor.

"In the bedroom." Monique's dreamy voice floated down.

He gazed at the portrait hanging on the wall. Jamal stood beaming in front of his mother and

Turning Around

stepfather. Monique's coils splayed on Justin's shoulder where she laid her head.

"Justin?"

"Comin'." He bounded up the stairs two at a time. Turning around in that emergency room was the best decision he ever made.

Something Special

SHORT STORY

LYNDELL WILLIAMS

Something Special

Get in the Car

"Subhanallah, Ma. Don't worry," Adeelah squeezed past the cluster of men rudely chatting at the large masjid entrance, "I just had to make salaah. I'm heading to the store now. Excuse me." She made sure they saw her exaggerated eye roll before rounding the huge embellished door and shooting onto the busy Atlantic Avenue sidewalk. Some brothers just had no home training.

People in thobes and jilbabs scurrying up and down the street and into and out of shops gave this section of Brooklyn a Middle Eastern tone, but the many races and ethnicities of the Muslims shopping for the upcoming 'Eid celebrations conveyed the diversity of the New York followers of the faith.

"*Do you have the list?*" Her mother's irritation transmitted clearly through the phone. Ironically, the last days of Ramadan made her and everyone else enduring weeks of fasting the most impatient.

"Yeah, you sure you don't want to leave some stuff for other people?" Adeelah snickered and ran her finger between her face and the edge of her khimar to allow a rare small breeze to flow inside.

"You're a real riot."

"I get if from you, mom." She wove through the crowd. There were quite a few stops to make. *Best to get this over with and off the streets.* "Oh, I also need to—" Her heart jumped. An icy chill shot through her body as a hand clamped on her shoulder. "Oh, no." She spun under its pull.

Taal peered at Adeelah; his smoke-grey eyes burned with rage. "Oh, yes. I got you now." Pain shot through her scalp where her husband grabbed a fist full of hair over its covering. Her head and neck snapped with every jerk. "I hear you think you're divorcing me."

Adeelah's survivor instincts kicked in; she dug her short nails into and scraped them down his hand, backing away the moment it opened. "I'm not staying married to you," she heaved and seethed through clenched teeth. "You're an animal."

The red flush covering Taal's screwed face matched the khimar crushed in his grip. He dropped it and stalked towards her, nostrils flared and a vein twisting down the front of his forehead. "That's not going to happen. You ungrateful bitch. Do you know what I've gone through to be with you? My family flipped when they found out I was marrying a Black. No one wants us around. Ever wonder why we're never invited to family gatherings? They even threatened to disown me, but I stood my ground."

Adeelah stumbled backwards. "I don't know why. Nothing I do is good enough." Flanked by the traffic-heavy street and stores, Taal scrambled to block her from any open doors. "You're always getting mad and beating on me. I'm not going to be your punching bag anymore. I don't care how many times you say sorry, I'm tired of a broken

Something Special

heart," she held up the arm that had been in a cast the week before, "and broken bones. I want you out of my life.

"You're not divorcing me after all I've done for you." Huge balled fists swung at the bottom of bulging arms. "You're mine!" His roar tore through the city din surrounding them and into her heart. Some pedestrians stopped while others simply glanced without pausing their progress. She winced under the vice-like grip of his hand around her wrist. He dragged and flung her onto a silver BMW. If only she'd noticed it earlier and had a chance to get away. "In the car, now." He swung the driver's door open.

Adeelah shot off the hood and bolted back towards the masjid. Surely there would be someone there to save her. "Help me!" The same group of men clustered at the door stared, slack jawed and motionless. Pain shot through her head and shoulders at the volley of punches Taal rained on them. She ducked her head under her arms and fell to the ground, curling her body into a 'c' shape—a position she'd learn to assume in their first year of marriage.

The man who once claimed to love her towered over her. "Get up." More blows fell. "I said get up you—"

Adeelah raised onto her hands and scanned to see what interrupted another of her husband's violent beat downs. His face pressed against the engraved masjid door, Taal unsuccessfully tried to buck a huge man off of him. Tattoos spread down from under a t-shirt and quaked over her rescuer's massive arm muscles. "Are you insane, man?" Green eyes flashing with anger captured her gaze. "You okay, sis?"

Adeelah gulped and nodded. "Yeah." Lifting off the sidewalk on achy arms, she staggered, stroking her waves. *Where is my khimar?*

"No!" Another roar from Taal made the hairs on the back of her neck stand on end. "You're not goin' anywhere." She spun to the scuffling.

Taal growled and sprung off the door; the large man subduing him stumbled back but caught his footing and swept a leg under her soon-to-be ex-husband's feet. "Oh, no you don't." The man straddled and held both of Taal's wrists with one hand. "*You're* not goin' anywhere." He sneered at the doorway trio. "One of you *men* call the police." The bass voice set the stagnant bunch in motion.

Something Special

Coffee for Iftar

One by one, the police cars clustered in front of the masjid began to roll away. Taal glared at Adeelah through the back window of the last cruiser to depart, his scowling visage shrinking as it crept through traffic. "Okay, ma'am." The short female officer grabbed her attention. "We're finished for now. Be safe."

"I will, thank you." Were things finished? Would there ever be a time she could actually just breathe and not have to worry about Taal's rage? Adeelah hugged herself with one arm and looked down at her mother's face shining under the web of her phone's shattered glass. "Just great."

"What's wrong?" Urban Lancelot leaned his head near hers, obviously avoiding any casual touching. Red brows shot up. "Oh, that's not good."

"No, it isn't. I could probably still use it, though." She sighed and strode down the street, skimming over bubblegum-stained concrete for a cherry-colored cloth. "Right now, I need my khimar." Her knight in shining blue jeans trailed her.

"I think I see it." He jogged a little ahead and bent at the curb. Full peach lips surrounded by a thick auburn beard pressed into a thin line. He presented the filthy garment. "This isn't good either."

Adeelah took the khimar, grunted and rubbed her pulsing temples. "Subhanallah." Her shoulders shook as she sniffed back all of the embarrassment, pain and regret loving the wrong man brought her. "I can't catch a break."

Wade dipped his head to get her attention and smiled. The oval, dark brown eyes brimming with tears sent a surge of concern through him. "Don't worry, sis. Allah is merciful, we can fix all of this." His heart skipped when her brown cheeks rose into orbs flanking full lips. He shifted his gaze to his sneakers.

"We?"

"Yes, we." He put a hand to his chest. "I can't just leave you like this." He turned his head up and down the street. "There." He pointed to a store with Islamic clothing hanging in the window and headed towards it. "Come on." He looked over his shoulder. The beautiful woman, pinned to her spot, fumbled the dirty khimar. He walked back and offered a reassuring grin. "I'm sorry. As salam alaykum. I'm Wade Reid. Please, let me help. I could use the blessings."

Her eyes softened. "Okay. Jazakallah. I'm Adeelah Yazdi—" she shook her head and grimaced, "I mean Bilal—Adeelah Bilal."

"Pretty name." Wade glanced at his phone and read *Diego* before tucking it into his front jean pocket. *He can wait.* "Let's go." They stepped into the store with Quran wafting through garments cascading from hooks near the ceiling. Air, balmy from incense and oils in glass cases and on shelves, greeted his nose. He stood opposite her at a long

Something Special

table hosting piles of folded khimars with a *Hijab* sign hanging from the ceiling.

"So," Wade jammed his fingers in his front jean pockets, "what would you like?" He smiled at the sunken head with soft, black waves flowing into a bun of coils at the base. *Damn. It's getting hard not to look. What is it about this woman?*

"At this point," she dug through the pile, "who cares?"

Her shaky tone tugged at him. She seemed strong and fragile at the same time. He plunged a hand into the soft fabric. This couldn't be easy for her. The covered Muslim women he knew went to great lengths to stay that way, and here she was with a bunch of strangers ogling her. He lifted a red folded scarf. "How about this one? It looks like what you have."

She snatched and opened the rectangular fabric, wrapping it around her head and neck. She looked up. "Sorry. Jazakallah." She pinned her shoulders back, searching her bag on her way to the cash register.

Wade dashed to meet her. "No," He pulled the wallet from his back pocket, "I'm paying."

The handbag she hiked up her shoulder swung at her hips. "You don't have to."

"But I want to."

"Jazakallah." She lifted her chin and disappeared through the shop door. Wade tossed a large bill on the counter and raced after the sister. There was something about her that called to him. He couldn't lose track of her. The tension in his neck eased when he saw her standing outside—the city darkening around her. The hem of her red skirt whipped around her ankles and shoes. The new scarf flew up in the breeze and brushed her cheek, making an already stunning women look like an ethereal beauty—irresistible to touch. But resist, he must. He sucked his teeth and dug his phone from his pocket. Diego's name appeared on the screen again. He grazed his thumb across the screen and began typing.

"It's almost maghrib," she announced in a calm voice.

He stopped. "Yeah, how about we find someplace to break our fasts? You wanna go to the masjid?"

"No."

He raised his eyebrows at the snap. "Okay, let's not go to the masjid."

She let out a heavy sigh. "Sorry," she shifted her gaze to the sidewalk. "I keep saying that, don't I?"

"It's alright. You've been through a lot." He tucked the phone away. "There's a coffee shop on the corner. How about we go grab something?" She chewed her lip. Was he coming off creepy? He read his phone.

Diego: *ASA I'm at the masjid. Where are you?*

WAS Heading to the coffee shop at the corner. Meet me there instead. Wade scratched the back of his head and returned his attention to Adeelah. "You must be hungry. I sure am."

She swayed and twisted the corner of her new khimar. "I don't know."

Something Special

"I'll sit at a different table. Just let me get you some food." He pulled his lips into a boyish grin. "A little coffee won't hurt, right?"

Her pouty lips twitched. "I guess it won't.

Something Special

Lady's Choice

Wade's stomach growled so loudly at the smell of coffee and pastries that his companion glanced downward and chuckled. "Long day of fasting getting to you, brotha?"

He rubbed it and stepped along with her on the line. The barista and glass case holding delectable treats seemed so far away. "Well, it's 16 hours. I guess you're not bothered at all?"

Adeelah turned and looked at him, an endearing glint of amusement in her eyes. "Oh, I'm starving." Her smile faded as she leaned to peer past his arm.

"Don't worry, sis. He's gone."

She straightened. "Bad habit, I guess. It comes after 2 years of—never mind."

"I doubt he made bail in the past 20 minutes. If he ever comes around, I'll handle him. I'm not going to sit by and let anyone hurt my Muslim sister."

"Yeah, well, you won't always be around."

"Maybe I will be." It made no sense, but the need to protect a woman he just met surged through him. He scratched at his tattoos when she began to stare at them. "I know, not very Muslimy. I got them before I converted."

Her eyes widened. "Oh, sorry, but I was just looking at that Celtic cross. Are you Irish?"

"No." He ran his fingers through his hair.

"No?" Adeelah gasped. "Does that mean—"

"Line's moving." He jerked his shirt sleeve; if only it could grow in length to cover the ink permanently staining his skin with a past he'd already purged. "You know what you want?"

"Yeah." She turned and leaned against the counter. "Hi, I'll take a large coffee, half and half, light sugar." She craned her head up towards the menu on the wall behind the clerk. "I also want a spinach and feta egg sandwich and a bear claw."

"That sounds good," Wade moved next to her and pulled out his wallet. "I'll have what she is but make that 3 sandwiches and no bear claw." He passed his debit card to the clerk and cocked an eyebrow at Adeelah's smirk. "What?"

Adeelah tittered. "Nothing, just respecting your appetite." She took the tray with her order.

Wade grabbed a couple of water bottles and sat at an adjacent table as promised. Adeelah perched in a chair, closed her eyes and raised her hands. He followed suit, resisting the temptation to wipe the tear meandering down her cheek when he finished his *dua*. He picked up and demolished half of the first sandwich in one bite. He met Adeelah's surprised expression.

"Wow."

He finished the sandwich and rubbed a napkin across his mouth. "I work up an appetite."

"May I ask doing what?" She made a dainty bite into her sandwich while he tore into his second.

"MMA fighting."

"Wait a minute," Adeelah laid her sandwich on the paper and pointed at him, her eyes enlarged with realization. "I've seen you on posters."

Something Special

"Yup." Her gaze traveled up and mouth hung opened as a baritone voice with a thick Spanish accent sprung from behind him. "He's an awesome fighter." Wade crammed the rest of his second sandwich in his mouth and stood to embrace Diego. "As Salam Alaykum."

"Wa alaykum salam. Diego Martir, this is Adeelah Bilal. She agreed to break fast with me."

"Really?" One could almost hear a *ting* as Diego flashed pearly-white teeth and a Hollywood smile. "What a kind woman to take pity on this sad, lonely man."

Adeelah beamed, bent her head and fiddled with the red fabric draped over the back of it. "I think he's nice."

Diego laughed "That he is. If you'll excuse me; I haven't broken my fast yet." He slipped between tables and stopped in front of the counter. His immediate effect on the simpering barista was apparent from across the shop.

When Diego returned with a heaping tray of food, Adeelah giggled and crossed her arms. "Let me guess, another MMA fighter?"

Diego cocked an eyebrow. "No, I'm an attorney." He removed his suit jacket; his muscular physique strained against a white dress shirt.

"Diego trains with me but doesn't fight." Wade crumbled the paper from the last sandwich. "He's too busy suing big bad corporations that hurt the little guy."

"Really," Adeelah slowly batted her dense eyelashes and played with the flap of her coffee cup, "that sounds so noble."

Diego smoothed his tie. "Mashallah, it can be very fulfilling."

"Your accent. Are you Puerto Rican?"

Diego raised his square chin and puffed his chest. "Sí, born and raised in Ponce. I'm impressed by your accuracy."

"Yeah, it's a gift."

It was hard not to notice the electricity surging between them. *I don't believe this. I fight off her jackass husband, and he just swoops in with his accent?* Wade drained the first water bottle.

Diego muttered a dua and began eating. "So, Adeelah, what do *you* do?"

Adeelah took a sip of coffee. "Presently, I'm serving as Wade's damsel in distress."

Diego stared at his friend. Wade slowly lowered his lids and shook his head. "I'm honored to be your hero." He rose. "Do you have a car? I'll walk with you." *Time to get her away from the Muslim Don Juan.*

"Don't worry. It's right across the street, and you've done so much already." She passed a hand over her khimar. "After all, you chased the dragon away, right?" She slowly blinked. "You're wonderful, Wade Reid."

Heat rushed up Wade's neck and face. The spark between them hadn't faded. He held out his hand. "Can I have your phone?" Confidence burgeoned

Something Special

through him when she obliged. "Here, call or text me to let me know you got home okay."

"Sure thing."

"If you don't mind." Diego popped a black business card between them. "I would also like to know you're safe and sound. Brothers must protect their sisters."

Wade glared at his soon-to-be former buddy.

"Thanks. Alhamdulillah. I guess I have two heroes now?" She rounded some diners and headed for the door. "As salam alaykum."

Wade dropped his forced smile as soon as she was gone. "Damn you and your corny accent, you—"

"Brother," Diego sat with a smug grin, "it's Ramadan. Why all the anger?"

Wade's seat creaked and shook under his weight. "I saw her first."

"Normally, I would respect that, but not with her. She's no ordinary woman."

"Yeah, I noticed," Wade's chair shot from under him and crashed into a couple of empty ones, "which is why I will not be bowing out gracefully." He picked up his tray and stormed to the trash can. They'd been fast friends since Diego moved to the city, but he was ready to rethink the whole brotherhood first idea for a girl like Adeelah.

Diego dumped the paper remains of his food and followed Wade outside. "How about we let the lady decide?"

"Fine." Wade's phone buzzed.

Lyndell Williams

Adeelah: *As Salam Alaykum. I'm in the car. Jazakallah for everything. I'll never forget how great you were to me. Let me know about your next fight. I think I might like to go.* ☺

Wade held the phone in front of Diego before tucking it into his pocket and spreading a triumphant smile across his face. "I think she's made her choice."

Something Special

A Little Won't Hurt

"Come on," Adeelah moaned, her body pressed against his brawny shoulder; she reached for the mug as best she could on her tiptoes. "Dr. Sharif said one cup was okay."

"I said no, Dee." Tan liquid splattered and flowed down the white granite sink. Diego put the mug inside and turned. "I heard you sneaking a cup earlier, which would've made *that* your second." He smiled down and kissed her. A swell of desire rose inside him. Ever since he saw her that evening in the coffee shop with Wade, she'd seized his heart and made it hers.

Adeelah lowered her lids and slid her arms around his neck. "You're cruel."

Diego smirked. "Don't be upset, cariño." He stroked the small mound in her tummy. "I'm thinking of you and our little one." He pressed his cheek against the bump, offering their unborn child some endearing Spanish words before straightening and rubbing the furrow between his wife's brows smooth. "Now," he pecked at her lips, "I'll get you something else, but no more coffee." The lingering sweetness fed his hunger for her.

Goosebumps raised down his neck where Adeelah's soft fingers stroked. "Well," she ran them through his curls, "I can think of something else." She claimed his mouth. Her silky tongue sliding against his made his blood course. She crushed her breast against him and traversed fingers down until she palmed the twitching and growing bulge in his pants.

He tore their kiss and filled his lungs. Her brown eyes sparkled with desire. It was so easy for her to bring him to distraction. "You're insatiable."

Adeelah tilted her head and raised her arched eyebrows. "You're complaining?"

Diego glanced at the microwave clock on the wall. They still had time. "Not at all." He covered his wife's mouth, slid his palms down her back and filled them with her spectacular round bottom. Adeelah yanked at the hem of his shirt and prodded him with her bulging belly. He walked backwards, guiding them to the bedroom, leaving a trail of clothes until he laid his beloved's nude body on the fluffy bed comforter—reveling in the bliss that only her touch gave him.

* * *

"As-salam alaykum?" Adeelah stretched her legs between the blankets and tucked the pillow further under her head. Her face tingled under the caress of Diego's calloused hand. "Mi amor? You need to get up to make dhuhr."

She lifted her heavy lids and smiled when her gaze focused on her husband's kind amber eyes. They were what she first noticed when he appeared behind Wade at the coffee shop. "Aight," she drawled and stroked his moist beard, "Give me a minute." The tender nips on her lips filled her with delight from head to toe.

Diego rose to his feet and adjusted the downy towel covering his torso; his light brown skin glistened in the sunlight. An Islamic lecture in Spanish drifted from his phone on the dresser.

Something Special

"Okay," he reached in a drawer and pulled out a pair of pants, "but don't take too long."

She squinted at the sun-soaked window, lifted on an elbow and tucked the blanket under her arm. "We still have some time before 'Asr," she glided her hand over his side of the bed, "sure you don't want to lay back down?"

Diego threw back his head and laughed before tugging on a t-shirt with *Boston College* imprinted across the front. "I love what those pregnancy hormones are doing to you, cariño," he sauntered to the edge of the bed and leaned over her, "but I can't. Wade will be here any minute."

She accepted another kiss before falling on her back, poking out her lips in feigned dejection. "Your loss, brotha."

Diego sniggered. "It truly is." He picked up his phone. The voice of the lecturer faded as her husband disappeared behind the bedroom door.

Adeelah giggled. He was such a blessing. She cast the comforter aside and scooched towards the edge of the bed. She stilled at the flutter tickling her insides—a reminder of another blessing and Allah's promise of double-ease after hardship. After almost a year of ordeal trying to get Taal out of her life, there was finally some equilibrium. Through all of it, Diego remained steadfast in his love for her.

Wade's booming salam filtered through the door as she waddled into the bathroom.

Something Special

Something Special

Diego coughed at Wade's hearty slap against his back. The bulking redhead kicked off his sneakers and made a beeline to the kitchen. "As-Salam Alaykum, man. The food ready?" He ducked into the refrigerator. "I'm starvin'."

Diego shook his head, skirted past his friend, and pulled a bag of tortilla chips from the oak cabinet. "Adeelah didn't start cooking yet." He tossed the bag in the air. "Here." His friend instinctively caught it.

Wade followed Diego into the living room. "What do you mean she didn't start cookin'? You invited me over for lunch." Wade fell silent, flashed his eyes and smirked as the soft hum of shower water permeated through the closed bedroom door. "I see." He flopped and propped a leg over an arm of the overstuffed side chair. "You couldn't let her make my mac and cheese first? It's why I trekked out here to the boonies." The bag popped open between Wade's burly hands. "I hate that long ride down the LIE."

"We're happy." Diego handed his best friend a bowl of salsa, "The further away from the city drama, the better." He sat on the edge of the sofa and turned the tv up loud enough to drown out the sound of the shower.

"Yeah," Wade talked between crunches, "Can't argue with that. After all the trouble Adeelah's ex caused, you two deserve some peace, inshallah."

Diego set his jaw. "Taal's not stirring up anything, is he?" He sat straight and reared his shoulders back. Every nerve prickled with the urge to protect Adeelah and the baby. "I won't have my wife upset by him again." He stood. "Perhaps I should speak to him."

Wade tossed the bag of chips on the walnut-stained coffee table and chortled. "Calm down, brother. No trouble." He continued as he licked each fingertip of his right hand. "Besides, I don't think it'll ever be necessary for you to *talk* to him again." He shot out of the chair with surprising ease for a man his size and carried the empty bowl to the kitchen. "You made things clear the last time." He dumped the bowl in the sink and grabbed the jar of salsa from the fridge. "Broken noses tend to do that."

Diego folded his arms. "He touched my Dee."

Wade reclaimed his seat and chips. "If I recall," he pointed a chip loaded with salsa at Diego, "you were only intended at the time." He twitched his bushy ginger eyebrows and shoved the food in his mouth. "I get it, though," he mumbled. "She's special. That's why I kept her with me that day Taal attacked her in front of the masjid. I knew there was something about her. When I saw how interested you became once you laid eyes on her, *mashallah*, I was sure I made a wise decision."

Diego gazed at the ceiling for thunderbolts. "That's the version you're sticking with, *amigo*?"

"Yup, Now, look at you two." Wade puffed his muscle-bound chest. "Married and about to have a baby."

"You must be so proud of your intuition."

Something Special

Wade jutted his bearded chin in the air. "I am, alhamdulillah. You can name the baby after me if it's a boy."

"Don't worry," Adeelah glided out of the bedroom; the hem of her denim skirt swished over her bare feet, "It's at the top of the boy's list." She greeted their guest, yanked up the sleeves of her emerald green long-sleeve tee and rounded the kitchen island. "Lunch won't be long. I'm not baking the mac and cheese."

Wade scowled at Diego. "See how you mess things up for me? Come on, sis. You gotta bake it."

"Next time, I promise," Adeelah said over clanking pots. "Sabr, brotha."

"Ugh," Wade dropped his head back, "fine. I still get salmon cakes though, right?"

"You got it. Diego, can you fill this pot for me?"

Diego patted Adeelah's bottom and took the pasta pot. "Sure." The geometric-patterned mint khimar made her brown skin glow. Hell would freeze over before he would allow Taal or anyone else make the content on her face fade.

Adeelah paused and grinned at the soft knocking sound coming from the front door. She caught Diego's gaze with her twinkling eyes. "Oh, that must be Lindsay."

"Lindsay?" He glanced at Wade emptying crumbs from the bag into his open mouth. "You invited her?"

"You're having a friend over, why can't I? Can you get the door, Wade?"

"'Kay." Wade tossed the empty bag on the island and bounded for the door.

Diego leaned in closer. "What are you up to?"

Adeelah grinned and began running a wedge of cheddar up and down the grater.

"As-salam alaykum." Lindsay's full lips formed a bright smile. She dropped her handbag on the floor and threw her arms up as she glided into the kitchen. "How are you feeling, sis?" She pat Adeelah's lower abdomen then frowned. "You're just getting started? Let me help."

"Jazakallah." Adeelah handed Lindsay the block of cheese and twirled towards the stove.

Diego left the kitchen, encountering Wade, beet-red cheeks over his beard and mouthing "who is that?" while pointing in Lindsay's direction.

He clamped a hand on Wade's neck. "Would you like to see if the ladies need some help?"

Wade glanced and smiled at the women. "It's only fair. We can't reinforce gender stereotypes, now can we?"

Diego laughed and turned his struck friend towards the marble-topped island. Lindsay, standing on the other side, soon put Wade to work. Although the fighter could easily take a man down, the pearl onions she passed him proved more challenging. He made quite the scene trying to peel back papery layers from the tiny bulbs with his meaty fingers and blushed every time one popped in the air from his strength. "I'm sorry," Wade furrowed his brows, "guess I'm not very much help."

Something Special

Lindsay giggled and picked up another onion that got away from the smitten man across from her. "Alhamdulillah, I think you're doing fine." She switched the bowl of onions for one containing fresh green beans and demonstrated snapping the ends to Wade. "It's always nice to see a man cooking."

Wade pulled his mouth into a half-smile and commenced with cracking the ends off the beans. "Honestly, I'm not a great cook," he looked at Lindsay, "but I'm willing to learn."

Lindsay slid the back of her hand across the beads of sweat on her forehead. Her umber skin brightened from the unseen blush underneath. "That's good to know."

Lunch became an early dinner filled with restrained flirting between the besotted duo as they sat in different parts of the open-concept apartment. The various shades of red Wade became when talking to Lindsay provided the meal's entertainment.

After Maghrib prayer, Adeelah and Diego waved from the door while Wade walked Lindsay to her car. "So," His wife smirked and squeezed his waist, "did he ask about her?"

Diego pinched Adeelah's bottom, delighted by her giggle as she rushed into the apartment. "Yes, but you knew he would, didn't you, mi amor?"

"I had a feeling." She unpinned her head covering, plopped her feet on the sofa and laid on a cushion. "Lindsay's special—smart, funny and inspiring in her love for the Deen. I just felt deep down that she would be perfect for him. Given the way he looked at her, I think I was spot on."

Diego put her head in his lap and loosened the mass of coils from the band restraining them. "Interesting, and exactly how did he look at her?"

She rubbed the bump and grinned ear to ear. "The same way you looked at me that day in the coffee shop."

Diego brushed Adeelah's pillowy lips with his. Alhamdulillah. She was truly a ni'mah.

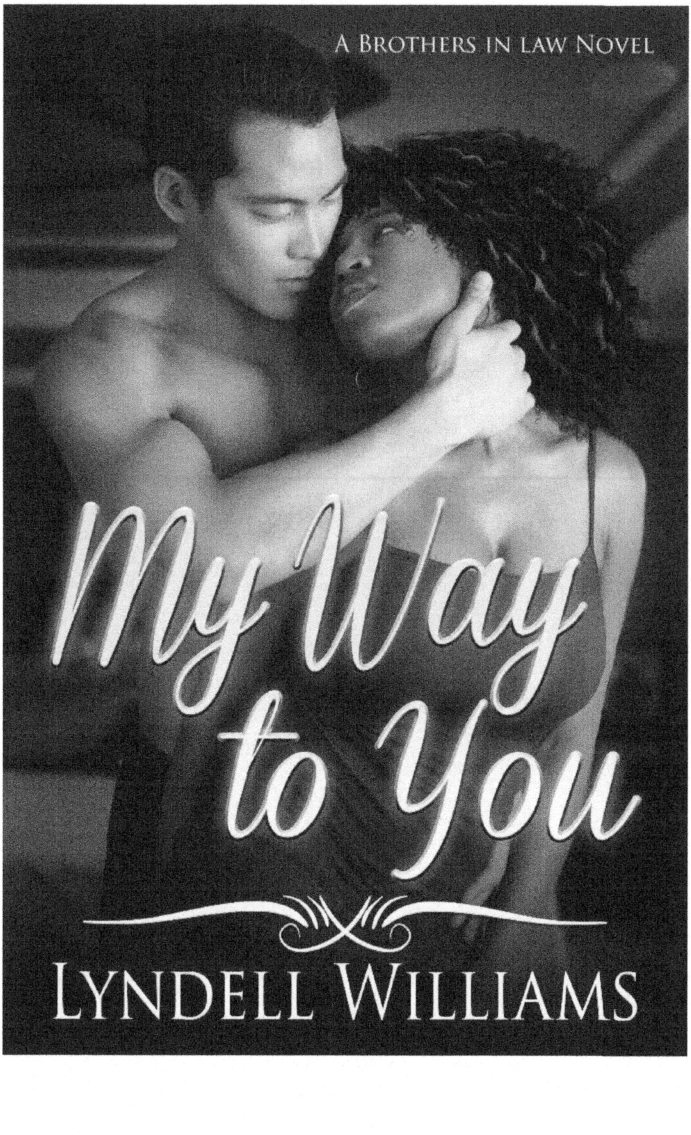
A BROTHERS IN LAW NOVEL
My Way to You
LYNDELL WILLIAMS

My Way to You

Brothers in Law, Book 1

Another night of passion is worth the risk.

Simon falls for Marcus' younger sister, Regina. Will big brother flip when he finds out that his best friend and a known playa is going for his sister? Regina is feelin' Simon too, but what will her pro-Black blog fans say about her dating and Asian man?

Chapter One - Back in New York

SIMON'S CHEST SWELLED as he let the box of books hit the wood floor with a loud thud. He surveyed his new digs. Although the Brooklyn Heights apartment was not the same as his mother's sprawling house in Jamaica Estates, it was good to be officially a New Yorker again. He achieved his goals in Boston, but his longing for home nagged him the entire four years he'd lived there. He also couldn't wait to get away from the pain and bad memories.

There wasn't much left to do in the apartment. Save for a few boxes and pictures leaning on the walls where they were to be hung, he was pretty much set. All the furniture was in place, the handiwork of his mother, who oversaw the deliveries like a drill sergeant. Alice Young had gotten straight to business. She made certain that her son's new abode was as comfortable and organized as his childhood home. Getting his bearings at the new law firm that recruited him after his first summer internship was challenging, and the last thing he had time for was to supervise painters and handymen. *I have to do something nice for her as soon as things settle down at work.*

He reached for the buzzing phone on the counter. "Hi, Ma." Simon pressed the phone against his ear and began stocking small jars from a bag on the floor into the empty refrigerator.

"*Hello, Simon. Are you all settled?*"

"Yes."

"*Did you put the kimchi in the refrigerator?*"

"I did." The last jar rattled against the rest. "Thanks for making them for me." He closed the refrigerator and rubbed his growling stomach. As good as his mother's *kimchi* was, he had a hankering for something else.

"*Of course. Let me know when you want more.*"

"Will do."

"I packed the rest of your things here. I can have them mailed to you."

"No, Ma. That's okay." Simon grabbed the keys off the counter and shoved his wallet into his jacket pocket. "I'll get them the next time I come out there."

"*I'll leave them in your old room then. Have you eaten?*"

My Way to You

"That sounds good." Simon stood in front of the entryway mirror, combing his fingers through the top of his hair, still amazed at how intuitive his mother was. "I'm going to get somethin' now." The soft click of the apartment door's lock echoed down the hall as he headed for the elevators.

"Eating out? You know you can't live like that, Simon. It's not healthy."

"I know, Ma. Don't worry. I'll go grocery shopping tomorrow. Lots of fruits and vegetables. I promise." He endured his mother's subsequent lecture about proper nutrition all the way to the subway platform, injecting the requisite yeses, confirming that he was dutifully listening. "Ma, I gotta go. I'll call you tomorrow?"

"I'm sure you will." Alice's tone conveyed the perfect combination of sarcasm and warning. *"But I'll be busy getting ready for my trip, so we can talk when I get back. Love you."*

"Okay, ma. Love you too," Simon shouted into the phone, unsure if she heard him over the screeching sound of the train.

❧❧❧❧

Simon weaved through the rows of tables, then sat and inhaled the glorious mixture of aromas wafting around him. He typed *I'm here, man* before setting down his phone. The tapestry of people testified to the popularity of Sylvia's Tiny Kitchen and proved that it was worth the subway ride from Brooklyn to dine. Sitting in the middle of the soul food restaurant reminded him of days spent travelling on the train across the city with his dad, who was a hard-core fan of the cuisine and passed it onto his son.

He raised his hand to catch the attention of a waiter. After weeks of newness, it was finally time to enjoy something that solidified that he was truly home. Just like the traditional Korean and Irish dishes served at the Young residence, the steaming plates at the Harlem landmark represented a staple of his life. He scanned the menu. *I want some catfish.*

"Welcome to Sylvia's. What would you like today?"

He opened his mouth to order but was interrupted by a voice from across the crowded restaurant. "Simon!" He turned, and his gaze fell upon two men weaving towards him. The tall, muscular man led the pair. His eyes flashed recognition: the corners of his mouth pulled back exposing shining white teeth. Simon bolted out of his seat and gripped the broad forearm.

"Hey, man." Familiarity fueled Simon's excitement at the sight of his best friend Marcus Kent's warm, brown face. He wrapped his free arm around the brawny man, giving as firm a squeeze as he got. Marcus stepped back, keeping one hand on Simon's shoulder.

"You look good, man. Did you have an easy time findin' the place?" Marcus's hand came down on Simon's shoulder in a few hearty pats.

My Way to You

"Please," Simon gave Marcus's bicep a playful jab, "I've been coming to Sylvia's since I was a kid. You're the Long Islander.

Marcus belted out a baritone laugh. "True. I hope you don't mind. I brought my intern." Marcus slapped the back of the young man next to him, whose head towered over even a man of his stature. "Simon, meet Jeremy Stacks. He's pursuing a future in law as well."

"Absolutely. Nice to meet you, Jeremy."

The waitress cleared her throat. Simon looked over to the woman standing, tapping her order pad. "So, that'll be three?" Her tapping moved from her pad to the floor with her foot.

"Yes, thank you," said Simon with a sheepish smile. The men sat and quickly ordered before returning to their conversation. Simon read his phone.

Missy: *How about we chill tonight?*

Simon: *Sure, I can't come until later tonight though.*

Missy: *I'll wait up.*

He smiled at the sexy picture that appeared on his phone.

"So," Marcus leaned back in his chair and smirked, "you still have the women fallin' all over you and that sexy Asian game of yours?"

Simon let out a soft chuckle. "I do aight. How's Toni?"

"She's good. Her practice is thriving. Now, let me guess, you're at that big law firm that was sniffing after you?"

"Pretty much. As I recall, the headhunters were chasing you big time too. Did you choose a firm?"

Marcus shook his head. "Nah, man. I decided against churning in the legal machine. I launched a small, multi-service not-for-profit. I want to make a direct difference for folks catching hell around here."

The waitress returned with drinks and bread. Simon bit pensively into a roll. "You always said you wanted to get involved in community organizing. I just thought it would be after you established a legal career."

Marcus took a long drink from his glass before setting it down. "Well, there are more than enough lawyers ready to work for rich folks. It's the poor who struggle for justice. Now I'm helping them with that struggle." The playfulness vanished from his eyes. "I remember when that was important to you as well."

Simon shifted in his chair. Marcus always shot straight from the hip and made no apologies. His former college roommate was particularly careful at making sure he didn't stray too far from his humanitarian commitments while he pursued success. "Yeah, it still is." The waitress placed the hot plates on the table. Simon reached for the pepper and sprinkled his catfish. "I haven't forgotten how important it is to give back. Didn't I always volunteer with you?"

Marcus grinned while he cut into the chicken in front of him. "Indeed, you did." He lifted the forkful of food and pointed it at Simon. "You stayed committed to whatever needed to be done. So, what are you doing to give back now?" The fork disappeared into his mouth.

A pang of guilt grew in Simon's stomach. "I haven't found an endeavor of interest," he said before putting his glass to his mouth.

Marcus's brows shot up. "Really? I find that surprising that no organization wants to avail themselves of someone as shrewd as you."

"Yeah, go figure." Simon chomped down on his fish. He shifted his gaze to Marcus's young companion, who he'd forgotten was even there. *Does he even talk? What am I gonna do? With this busy schedule of mine, I never considered volunteering anywhere, but Marc is right.* "Maybe," Simon raised his eyebrows at Marcus, "there's something I can do for you?"

Marcus lifted the napkin from his lap and wiped his fingers. "We do offer free legal services. Would you be interested in volunteering?"

"Definitely. Where are you located?"

A card appeared from Marcus's shirt pocket. "Harlem." He dropped it on the table next to Simon's plate. "We've a committee that meets once a month to strategize about initiatives and funding. I think it would be a good idea for you to come and sit."

"Sounds good." Pulling the wallet from his jacket, Simon shoved Marcus's card in before retrieving his. "But I'll need two or three weeks before committing to anything. I'm still gettin' my bearings at work."

Marcus flipped Simon's card front and back before placing it into his shirt pocket. "Uh-huh." He jabbed at his plate until his fork was refilled. "You were always organized and quick on the uptake. Unless things have changed, I'm sure you already have your bearings." The last mound of food disappeared, and Marcus signaled for the check.

Simon rubbed the back of his neck. Marcus made it obvious that he would not be put off and expected a shorter time frame for his friend to join him in the cause. "One week?"

Marcus slammed his hand on the table as he rose, rattling the plates and glasses. "Great. I knew you still had it in you. We're meeting this Thursday at 7:30."

"That's not one week."

"The address is on the card." Marcus thanked the waitress and grabbed the check.

"No, Marcus. I got it." Simon attempted to take the small slip from his friend, but it was moved out of his reach.

Marcus surveyed the check, then pulled a bunch of bills from his wallet. "Too late," he smiled at the waitress, "Keep the change."

The waitress's eyes lit at Marcus's generosity. "Thank you, sir. Enjoy your evening."

Stuffing his wallet into his back pocket, He looked down at Simon with a smug grin. "I plan to."

Jeremy reminded the men of his existence by rising and standing behind Marcus. "It was nice

My Way to You

meeting you," the young man said pushing his glasses up his nose. Was this the future of law? His face was so smooth, it indicated that shaving wasn't even necessary.

"So, Simon. I'll see you on Thursday?"

Simon raised his hands in defeat. "I'll put it on my schedule."

Marcus clamped down onto the back of his neck like when they were in college. "I knew you would. Great seein' you, bro." The two men weaved their way out of the restaurant and disappeared into the street.

Simon asked the waitress to put the rest of his meal in a to-go container and headed for the subway. A series of notifications—each containing an image of his *friend* in fewer clothes—reminded him that he wasn't going straight home to Brooklyn and needed to take different train.

꧁꧂꧁꧂꧁꧂꧁꧂

The following morning, Simon strode through the maze of cubicles. His black leather backpack flung behind his back, he navigated the twists and turns while balancing not one but two coffee cups. It only took a couple of weeks for him to devise a system to efficiently navigate through the entire building, which involved walking past the right offices while avoiding others.

"Good morning, Agnes," Simon smiled at the executive assistant for one of the senior partners, tilting his coffee in celebration of the day.

"'Morning, Simon."

Lyndell Williams

The matronly-dressed woman's smile revealed a set of highly polished dentures. Simon was always generally cordial to people, but he made it a special point to charm the firm's staff. It never hurt to have them on your side.

He turned a corner. His assistant, Corella was working at her desk.

"Good morning, Corella." His face beaming like a schoolboy with an apple for the teacher, Simon presented a coffee cup to her. "Two creams, no sugar."

Corella pulled off her reading glasses. "Thanks, Simon."

He dipped his head. "You're welcome." He stood in front of the desk, immobile, while his assistant checked out the caffeinated morning libations.

Corella's nose crinkled a little. She sniffed, carefully took one sip and smiled "You didn't have to."

Simon turned on his heel. "But I did." He strutted into his office.

She was the best assistant the firm had to offer. Years working with attorneys from associates to senior partners not only meant she had tons of experience but knowledge of the firm's inner workings. She knew where the bodies were buried. As a result, many feared her, but more so, they respected her.

She was valued enough at the firm that she could choose her own assignment. Simon was fortunate. Corella had tired of working with the last attorney and was looking to team up with another when he started. She selected him after a 10-minute conversation in his office. She was smart, organized, and efficient, and he did his best to make sure that she knew he appreciated her hard work.

Simon sat at his office desk. It was a small but respectable workspace. One wall hosted built in shelves and a closet, where he kept extra clothes. His L-shaped desk held his computer and a few drawers. On one side of the desk was his chair and opposite it was another for clients. It was a lot better than being stuck in the maze of cubicles, and there was a huge window that let in plenty of light.

Simon hung his jacket on the back of the door, sat at his desk and rolled his sleeves.

"Simon?" Corella called from the doorway, concentrating on her tablet screen.

"Yes, Corella?"

Without looking, she glided to the front of his desk. "I have an email you sent me yesterday. You need to clear part of your afternoon schedule one Thursday a month?"

Oh boy, Marcus. Simon scratched his head and swung his chair back and forth. "Yes, I'm going to be doing some pro-bono work for an organization in Harlem."

Corella's groomed brows drew close together as she looked up from her tablet.

"It's important. I just need to switch my schedule around to accommodate leaving an hour early on some Thursdays."

"Okay." Corella returned her attention to the screen. "That can be arranged. What's the name of the organization?"

Simon stood. He pulled out and searched his wallet. Retrieving Marcus's card, he held it in front of himself and tilted his head.

"May I see the card?" Corella held out her hand. "I'd like to enter the information in your contacts."

"Sure." Simon smiled and took a deep breath. "Thanks."

"You're welcome." Corella slowly disappeared behind the closing office door.

Simon reclined in his chair and stared at the ceiling. *Good thing Corella reminded me about Thursday. There's no way I would ever flake on Marcus—not after everything he's done for me. Besides, it's high-time I started giving back again.*

He punched the numbers on the desk phone to cease the red light flashing on it. He stiffened at the high-pitched saccharine voice in the first voicemail.

Hi, Simon. He peered at the wall hanging of a black figure brandishing a swivel chair like a sword. *I'm in New York, and I was hoping we could catch up.*

A knot twisted at the base of his neck and his heart raced out of control. Shutting his eyes, he hit the erase key and inhaled until the beating settled.

My Way to You

Get your copy of *My Way to You* today!

Visit
https://www.amazon.com/dp/B084Z6Q23W

A Brothers in Law Novel

Sweet Love Bitter Fruit

Lyndell Williams

Sweet Love – Bitter Fruit

Brothers in Law, Book Two

Marcus loves making Toni happy. He knows what to do to make her laugh with happiness and moan with desire. The passion between them is fully ablaze until she asks him to do something that can tear their happiness apart.

Chapter One Doctor's Office

MARCUS LOOKED AT ANOTHER HUGE BELLY passing in front of them and glanced at Toni. Being around so many pregnant women couldn't be easy for her. They had tried and failed so many times to have a baby. She sat poised and beautiful, flipping the pages of a magazine with her tapered fingers, garnering the usual admiring looks when they were in public. He tucked her swaying black bobbed hair behind an ear. He was damn lucky she gave him the time of day that afternoon at his parents' house. When their gazes met, he had become hooked, determined to make her his.

He glanced down at the diamond ring and smiled—mission accomplished. "You alright, babe?" he asked wrapping an arm around her shoulders.

Lyndell Williams

She lifted her head and smiled. "I'm fine," she looked around the waiting room, "a bit nervous. Inow I shouldn't be. This isn't our first time doing this." He stroked her cheek. Toni Kent was not the nervous type. She was typically the one making everyone else feel better. The tiny bulge at the top of her jaw twitched, lips pursed, clear signs that she was more than a little scared but not admitting to it. "It's going to be fine." Her round, brown eyes softened, melting his heart and steeling his resolve.

Her full brown lips spread into an electrifying smile as she lowered and raised her lids, stroking his arm. "Okay."

He hugged her, kissing her forehead as she laid her head on his chest. He really didn't want to do more in vitro treatments. The previous ones were disastrous, and this new round promised more of the same. He buried his nose in her hair and inhaled the floral scent, scanning the room full of guts and strollers. It meant so much to her that he couldn't bring himself to say no despite the word pounding through his head.

He held her tighter. Their experience had not been like what they saw in the brochures and books with pictures of smiling couples, pregnant women and mothers holding their newborns. A pit grew in his stomach. She may be ready for this, but he sure as hell wasn't.

"Toni? Toni Kent?" They stood. Keeping his hand at the small of her back, they walked up to the nurse in aqua scrubs. "Hi, I'm Laura." The tiny redhead smiled. Another beaming face masking the torment on the other side. "Follow me, please." The pit grew inside of him as she led them through halls and to an examination room.

Laura puttered around, the patronizing smile and wrinkle in the middle of her nose never leaving her face as she opened draws and cabinets. "Step on the scale, please, Toni." He sat and waited. The familiar sounds of the clanking scale and hissing blood pressure machine played a torch song that fed the sense of failure looming in his head.

"So, you guys are here because your last in vitro treatment didn't work?" asked Laura, scribbling across the open folder in her hand.

"Yes," Toni said, crossing her arms and dipping her head. Even the professionals didn't get how anxiety-ridden all of this was, at least not all of the time. He tilted his, winking when she met his gaze. A little more air entered his tight chest at the sight of the corners of her mouth twitching.

"All right. I guess you know the drill by now." Laura held up a folded paper gown. "Dr. Algiers will be in shortly," was the last thing she said before disappearing behind the door.

Toni undressed and climbed back up on the table. It was the same routine they had endured for months. He moved back and forth on the stool, staring at Toni's feet as she scrunched and flexed her painted toes reflecting the florescent lighting from the ceiling. His phone buzzed. He flew his hand to a pants pocket, taking it out and silencing the sound echoing off the cream walls decorated with charts revealing more then he wanted to know about the female anatomy.

Toni pursed her lips. "You can answer it, Marc. I'm not going to blow up at you."

He rose from the stool and nudged it backward with the back of his knees. He could smell the set up a mile away. There was no way he was falling into that trap. "Nope. This is more important. I want to focus." He rubbed at the goose pimples running up her arms. "Why do they keep it so damn cold in here?"

"I guess they want to keep the eggs fresh." He threw his head back and laughed. Good, a little bit of his Sweetness was breaking through the stress. She wrapped her arms around his neck. "Thank you for being so patient with my moodiness. I know it's been all over the place."

He squinted. "What, you?" He pressed their lips together, making bumps on his arms that matched hers. "You've been fine." A huge lie. She had been far from fine. Their home, the place where he found peace from the world, became a hormonal war zone with Toni primed for battle. It had gotten to the point where he either hid at work or the gym waiting out her latest mood shift, but fat chance that he was going to let her know how much it drained him. He was her husband—her rock, which meant sucking it up and taking whatever it was she had in her arsenal, including biting his head off over the slightest thing like leaving a cup in the sink or socks on the bathroom floor.

Her lips twitched with his. "You're lying," she smoothed her fingertips along the back of his head, "and I appreciate it. But let's be honest. These past few months took a lot out of us."

He encircled her waist. "I can't argue with that, but we managed our way through it, and will again." He reclaimed her lips and pulled her closer. The world, problems past and present faded. He always found so much happiness in her arms.

There was a soft knock at the door. Dr. Algiers glided inside and stood next to him. Even with a bun at the top of her head, it barely reached his armpit. "Okay, are you two ready?" she asked grinning and shifting her gaze between them. She rarely smiled, so seeing one pushing up her diamond cheeks allowed some reassurance to settle around him. Maybe things weren't as grim as they seemed.

He stared at Toni, wide-eyed and chewing the bottom of her lip. He took her shaking hands in his. This had to work.

Get your copy of *My Way to You* today!

Visit https://www.amazon.com/dp/B07WZ9LT97

About Lyndell Williams

Lyndell Williams has a B.A. in Historical Studies and Literature, M.A. in Liberal Studies, and an AC in Women and Gender Studies. She presently teaches history as an adjunct instructor.

Williams a cultural critic with a background in literary criticism specializing in romance. She is the managing editor of the NbA Muslims blog on Patheos and a writer for Haute Hijab and About Islam.

She received 2017 The Francis Award from The International Association for the Study of Popular Romance (IASPR). Her peer-reviewed journal article *The Stable Muslim Love Triangle – Triangular Desire in African American Muslim Romance Fiction* was published in the Journal of Popular Romance Studies November 2018.

Lyndell has contributed to multiple anthologies interracial short story collections, including - *Saffron: A Collection of Personal Narratives by Muslim Women*, *Shades of AMBW* and *Shades of BWW*

Made in the USA
Las Vegas, NV
31 July 2021